HIS SKIN WAS THE COLOR OF POND ALGAE . . .

"One, two . . . " Ellie whispered. She looked at Andy, and he put his hand on the doorknob of the bathroom. "Three!"

Andy flung open the door, and Ellie rushed into the bathroom.

"Aaaaa . . . aaaa!" she screamed.

In the middle of the bathroom, standing in a puddle of water, was the most hideous creature Ellie had ever seen.

Spike, she thought in disbelief.

There was no doubt about it. The *thing* that ogled at her through shining red eyes looked exactly like Hans's dead fish, Spike.

Only bigger—much bigger.

Read these other BONE CHILLERS **from HarperPaperbacks:**

BONE CHILLERS

TOILET TERROR

Created by
BETSY HAYNES

Written by
ELIZABETH WINFREY

HarperPaperbacks
A Division of HarperCollinsPublishers

This is a work of fiction. The characters, incidents, and
dialogues are products of the author's imagination and are not to
be construed as real. Any resemblance to actual events or persons,
living or dead, is entirely coincidental.

HarperPaperbacks   *A Division of* HarperCollins*Publishers*
10 East 53rd Street, New York, N.Y. 10022

Copyright © 1996 by Betsy Haynes and
Daniel Weiss Associates, Inc.

Cover art copyright © 1996 Daniel Weiss Associates, Inc.

All rights reserved. No part of this book may be used or
reproduced in any manner whatsoever without written
permission of the publisher, except in the case of brief
quotations embodied in critical articles and reviews. For
information address Daniel Weiss Associates, Inc., 33 West 17th
Street, New York, N.Y. 10011.

First printing: August 1996

Printed in the United States of America

HarperPaperbacks and colophon are trademarks of
HarperCollins*Publishers*

❖ 10 9 8 7 6 5 4 3 2 1

Chapter

It was Sunday afternoon, and Ellie Volkhausen sighed deeply when she heard her seven-year-old brother, Hans, call her name. She carefully set down the test tube full of blue liquid that she'd been studying and frowned. As usual, Hans had managed to break her concentration.

"Ellie! Ellie! Come *here!*" he yelled again.

She rolled her eyes in exasperation, as she did at least once a day. Since both Mr. and Mrs. Volkhausen had full-time jobs, it was Ellie's family duty to baby-sit her brother after school every day. And whenever else they couldn't be at home.

Ellie took a last look at her latest chemistry experiment. "I'll be there in a sec," she called back, slipping off the rubber gloves she wore whenever she handled chemicals.

Ellie headed down the hall, wondering what minor crisis her little brother had invented this time. *Was I ever such a pest?* she asked herself silently.

For almost as long as Ellie could remember, she'd needed only one thing to make her happy— a chemistry set. Now that she had turned twelve and entered the sixth grade, her parents allowed her to mix and match chemicals without their direct supervision. They knew Ellie was always careful, and she took science safety very seriously.

Ellie pushed open Hans's bedroom door and glowered at her little brother. "What is it now?" she asked.

As much as she sometimes wished her brother didn't exist, Ellie had to admit that looking at him was like seeing a younger, male version of herself.

They both had curly blond hair and light blue eyes, as well as the kind of chubby cheeks that old women liked to pinch. Ellie usually pulled her long curls back with a rubber band, although her mother was constantly giving her pastel ribbons to use instead. At the moment Hans's hair stuck out in all directions, and there was a smudge of dirt on his nose.

"Spike is dead!" Hans wailed, pointing at the fish tank in the corner of his messy room.

Ellie walked over to the tank. Sure enough, Hans's rumble fish, Spike, was floating belly up at the top of the fish tank. "Yep, Mr. Spike has done his last lap around his plastic castle," Ellie observed.

A tear ran down Hans's face. He reached into the tank and ran his finger over Spike's bloated body. "He was the best fish in the whole world." Hans let out a little sob, and his bottom lip began to tremble. "I'll miss Spike so much."

Ellie snorted. "What's to miss? All that fish ever did was knock his head against the side of the tank and stare at you with those beady little eyes."

Hans cried harder, pressing one tear-stained cheek to the glass of the tank. "You don't know anything! You don't care about anything but dumb old science!"

Ellie pulled Hans away from the tank and grabbed the small net that her mother used to clean the water. "Calm down, pest. Getting hysterical isn't going to bring Spike back to life."

Hans gazed forlornly at the motionless fish as Ellie caught Spike's small body in her net. "What will?" he asked.

Ellie wrinkled her nose. Fish were naturally smelly, and being dead didn't help the odor any. "What will what?" she asked.

Hans jumped up and down, trying to get a good look at the net, which Ellie was holding just above his head. "What will bring him back to life?"

Ellie raised her arm so that the fish was far out of Hans's range. "Nothing. At least, nothing that's been invented yet."

"Can we save him until something *is* invented?" Hans asked, his blue eyes wide and red from crying.

Ellie laughed. "Mom and Dad wouldn't appreciate that too much—although I could have a breakthrough with my heart-regenerating serum any day now."

Ellie was convinced that any day she would discover a liquid mixture that could restart a stopped heart. Her goal was to bring the dead back to life and to win the Nobel Prize for medicine.

Hans never doubted Ellie. "Really?" he asked, looking quizzical.

She nodded. "If a certain little brother would let me alone for two seconds at a time."

Remembering that her chemistry experiment was waiting for her, Ellie turned quickly. She wanted to get rid of Spike and get back to her work.

"Where are you going?" Hans asked, following at her heels as she walked out of his bedroom.

4

Ellie stopped quickly and Hans bumped into her. She waved the net in his face. "I'm going to give Spike a burial at sea," she said.

Hans looked puzzled. "But the ocean is far away! How are we going to get there?"

"You'll see," Ellie said. She continued down the blue-carpeted hall toward the bathroom that she and Hans shared.

Suddenly Hans seemed to understand what she was planning to do with the remains of his fish. "NO!" he screamed, tackling Ellie from behind.

Ellie stumbled and almost lost her hold on the net. With her free hand she gently shoved Hans back toward his bedroom. "Ellie, please!" he cried. "Let's bury Spike in the backyard, next to the pool. We can have a funeral, and build a grave, and . . . "

Ellie opened the door of the bathroom. "Do you know how deep we'd have to bury him to keep some dog or cat from digging him up and eating him?"

Hans's face paled. "Eating Spike?" he squeaked.

"Yum, yum," Ellie said. "In fact, maybe I'll fry him up myself."

"No, no, no!" Hans shouted, lunging toward her.

Ellie dodged his body and backed into their bathroom. The small room was covered with aqua green tiles. At one end of the bathroom was a combination bathtub-shower with a sliding glass door. Ellie went to the toilet, which matched the aqua green of the floor and walls, and lifted the lid.

"Sure you don't want to eat him for dinner?" Ellie asked, dangling the fish's limp body over the toilet bowl. She put her hand on the flusher.

Hans tugged on the bottom of Ellie's blue-and-white-striped T-shirt. "El, will you at least say a prayer or something for him?"

Ellie's heart softened as she looked at her little brother's sad face. "Spike was a good fish," she began, feeling silly. "He will be missed by Hans Volkhausen. We wish Spike the best as we send him back to where he came from. So long, Spike."

With that Ellie dropped the dead fish into the toilet bowl. Her eyes stayed glued to the small body as it was tossed around and around in the swirling water. Then, with a final *whoosh*, Spike was sucked out of their lives forever. At least, that's what Ellie thought as she watched him disappear.

Chapter

An hour later Ellie handed a pair of safety goggles to her best friend, Andy Stein. They stood side by side in front of Ellie's lab table, looking at the jars and test tubes that Ellie had laid out.

"If this thing works, you'll be famous," Andy said, grinning widely to show the metal bands of his braces. He put the big plastic goggles on over his own horn-rimmed glasses.

The different shades of brown in Andy's glasses matched the chestnut of his straight brown hair. Although she knew Andy felt self-conscious about being a "four eyes," Ellie liked the way Andy's glasses highlighted his hazel eyes. They made him look like a professional scientist.

Ellie's blue eyes sparkled. "Nobel Prize, here I come."

"Explain the whole idea to me again," Andy suggested. "I'm still a little confused." He studied the warning label on a bottle of bromide. "Do you really think you have a chance to discover something important?"

Ellie shrugged. "Sure. Why not?" She took the bromide from Andy and put a dropper into the thin neck of the bottle.

"Well, so far you haven't come up with anything different from what we've done in science class."

"That's why I've got to keep trying," Ellie said.

Andy picked up a test tube and hesitantly sniffed the liquid inside. "You're just desperate for something interesting to happen. You'd probably be happy if you managed to blow up your house."

"Yeah, right. My parents would kill me—if the explosion didn't," Ellie responded.

She frowned at the small jar of liquid. Sometimes Andy had absolutely no faith. He thought she was just another amateur scientist playing around in her bedroom. But Ellie was sure that she had a certain power over chemicals—at least, someday she would.

"You're right about one thing," Ellie continued a moment later.

"What's that?" Andy asked. He sniffed at the chemicals, wrinkling his nose.

"Life has been pretty boring lately. Aside from chemistry, of course."

Andy laughed. "Oh, of course. No matter what, you've got science."

Ellie ignored his teasing. She was used to Andy making fun of her. "But there is something in the air. I think there are extra ions floating around. Or charged electrodes. Or something."

"Smells like stinky sulfur, if you ask me," Andy said.

Ellie shrugged. "Make as many jokes as you want. Something *big* is about to happen." She picked up a test tube and swirled the liquid inside. "I can just feel it."

Chapter

3

Ellie squirted lemon juice over the salmon pancakes her mother had brought home for dinner. Hans, understandably, had chosen to have a peanut butter sandwich.

Mrs. Volkhausen poured Hans a glass of milk and cleared her throat. "Ellie, honey, I know it's still hot as blazes outside, but autumn is just around the corner. Why don't we go shopping for some new school dresses for you?"

Ellie swallowed her salmon and gave her mother a suspicious glance. "I don't need any new clothes—especially not *dresses*."

Mrs. Volkhausen raised an eyebrow at her husband. "There's nothing wrong with wearing a dress, sweetie."

Ellie rolled her eyes. "Nothing wrong with wearing jeans, either."

Mr. Volkhausen grinned at Ellie, then turned to Hans. "Sorry about Spike, kiddo. But your sister said you handled yourself like a real trooper."

Hans looked hopefully in Ellie's direction. "She did?"

Ellie waved a piece of salmon in front of his nose. "Yeah, right!"

"Ellie, sticking pieces of fish in your little brother's face is *not* good manners," Mrs. Volkhausen said reproachfully.

Ellie popped the bite of salmon into her mouth. "Sorry, Mom."

"Speaking of manners, I have a *great* idea," Mrs. Volkhausen said, beaming.

Ellie gulped. She knew the look on her mother's face. It was the one Mrs. Volkhausen wore when she was about to suggest cheerfully that the whole family spend a Saturday morning raking leaves, or cleaning the garage, or waxing the car.

"What is it?" Ellie asked warily.

"Ballroom-dancing lessons," Mrs. Volkhausen said brightly.

"What?" Ellie shrieked. She reached over and pinched Hans, who was giggling around a mouth full of peanut butter.

11

Mrs. Volkhausen cut serenely into her fish. "The school newsletter announced a special dance class being offered for all the boys and girls in your class—Tuesday evenings, starting next week."

"No way, Mom!" Ellie shouted, feeling slightly panicky. She could just see herself stuffed into an ugly, frilly, ultra-starched dress, stepping on some horrible guy's toes.

"Dancing is great exercise, don't forget," Mr. Volkhausen said smoothly.

Ellie stuck out her tongue. "I get plenty of exercise from swimming—right in our own backyard. I don't need nasty *dance* lessons." She sighed. "Jeez!"

"Calm down," Mrs. Volkhausen said, an amused smile on her face. "Just promise me you'll think about it."

"If I promise to think about the class, can I be excused?" Ellie asked, trying to keep her voice neutral. "I want to keep working on my experiment."

"Sure, sweetie," Mrs. Volkhausen responded.

Ellie picked up her plate to carry it to the kitchen. As she pushed open the swinging wood door that separated the dining room from the kitchen, she heard her father's voice behind her. "Be careful with those chemicals, Madame

12

Scientist. We don't want you creating a monster up there."

Upstairs, Ellie slipped on her goggles and looked at her experiment. A gooey mass of blue-green mush oozed over the side of one test tube. Ellie squinted at her creation. During dinner the substance had turned into a kind of Day-Glo oatmeal. And the smell wafting toward Ellie's nose was a cross between cabbage cooking and a baby's dirty diaper.

"Great," Ellie muttered, plugging her nostrils between her thumb and index finger. "Two experiments ruined in one day."

She turned her attention to a small jar next to her Bunsen burner stove. Ellie observed about an inch of milky white liquid in the jar. When she'd gone downstairs for dinner, the liquid had been clear. *Must be the sulfate,* she thought.

Ellie sucked in a deep breath through her mouth, then unplugged her nose. With one hand she picked up the small jar and with the other she carefully took up the test tube. Holding both containers at arm's length in front of her, she headed out of her room and down the hall to the bathroom.

"Oomph!" Ellie yelled suddenly. She tripped over a small foot, losing her balance.

13

She fell onto her knees, still holding the chemicals high above her head. Out of the corner of her eye she saw Hans's guilty smile.

"Sorry, El," he said.

Ellie struggled to her feet. "You're lucky I didn't spill chemicals in your eyes," she said, shaking her head. "You'd be blind by now."

Hans backed against the wall. He seemed to want to be as far away from Ellie's failed experiment as possible. "Keep that stuff away from me," he whined.

Ellie stuck out her foot to threaten Hans with a kick in the shin. As he jumped back Mrs. Volkhausen's voice came from downstairs. "Ellie! Hans! What's going on up there?" she called.

Ellie glowered at her little brother. "Nothing, Mom. I'm just getting rid of some chemicals," she yelled.

Hans kept close to Ellie as she entered the bathroom. "Can I watch, Ellie?" he asked, hanging back at the door of the bathroom.

Ellie motioned him forward. "Do I have a choice?"

Hans knelt next to the toilet, and Ellie prepared to make a big show of getting rid of her useless chemicals. "Be careful not to breathe it in," she warned. "This stuff is dangerous."

Hans nodded solemnly, his eyes wide. "Now watch carefully," Ellie instructed. "When the chemicals from these different containers mix together, there's going to be a reaction."

Ellie poured the contents from the test tube and the beaker into the toilet bowl water. As the chemicals dissolved, the water turned a deep purple. Small bubbles rose to the top, fizzing at the surface.

"Wow," Hans said softly.

"Yeah. Wow." For once Ellie agreed with her little brother. Ellie flushed the toilet. The chemicals swirled around and around in the bowl, just as Spike had earlier. When the last of the purple water was sucked into the pipes, Ellie shut the lid of the toilet. "One more experiment down the drain," she joked.

"That was cool," Hans said.

Ellie ruffled his hair. Maybe there was still hope that she'd turn Hans into a fellow science nerd. "If you think *that* was cool, wait until I come up with an experiment that does more than turn purple."

Suddenly her smile faded. A loud, strangled gurgling sound came from somewhere deep in the toilet. Hans jumped back. "What was *that*?"

Ellie lifted the toilet lid and peered inside.

15

Nothing looked out of the ordinary. *Probably just the pipes settling or something,* she told herself.

But when she remembered the strange sound, she felt her heart sink a little. Was it possible that *her* chemicals had caused that noise? And if so, what did it mean?

Chapter

4

*T*he university auditorium was packed with men and women wearing suits and lab coats. From her chair onstage Ellie could see her mom, her dad, and Hans waving from the front row. Behind them were her grandparents, along with Andy and her sixth-grade teacher, Mrs. Mitchell.

Ellie smiled broadly as she waved back. Today was her day. After hundreds of failed experiments she'd finally made her breakthrough. Ellie's heart pounded as she watched a gray-haired, wise-looking professor walk slowly to the podium at center stage.

As the old professor tapped on the microphone the crowd in the auditorium grew quiet. "Ladies and gentlemen, it is my pleasure to introduce a girl who has changed the face of modern medicine."

The sound of applause rose throughout the auditorium. Ellie's mother was smiling so widely that her face looked as if it would break in two.

"This girl has single-handedly given us the power to bring back the dead," the professor continued. "Her heart-regenerating serum is what some might call a miracle."

Again loud applause rippled through the audience. Tears glistened in Ellie's eyes as she thought about the prize she was about to receive.

"Please join me in congratulating Ellie Volkhausen, the youngest person ever to receive the Nobel Prize in medicine," the professor finished.

Ellie's legs shook as she walked toward the podium. When she reached center stage, she stood on her tiptoes so that she could reach the microphone. "Thank y—"

Her words were cut off by a loud banging at the auditorium doors. All heads turned to the back of the room, where a door was slowly opening.

Ellie stood rooted to her spot on the stage as a shadowy figure appeared in the auditorium. The sound of banging continued as Ellie's blood ran cold.

The figure stepped into the light, and suddenly she was staring into the glowing eyes of a monster. His long body was a combination of pukey green and ashy black, coated all over with thick wet slime. From inside his huge, fang-toothed jaw a pointed red tongue flicked in and out. The monster came closer. . . .

Ellie's eyes opened wide as she awoke from her nightmare. Drops of sweat ran down her face. After a few seconds Ellie realized that the pipes of the Volkhausens' house were banging loudly.

Feeling foolish, Ellie flopped onto her stomach and gave her pillow a soft punch. The ominous sounds that had disturbed her perfect dream hadn't come from a monster—the banging had been nothing more than faulty plumbing.

Chapter

"**H**urry, Ellie! I have to *go*," Hans said Monday after school.

Ellie slowly turned the key in the lock of the Volkhausens' front door. "I'm not letting you in until you promise to give me some peace and quiet this afternoon."

Hans jumped up and down. "Cross my heart," he promised.

Ellie pushed open the door and allowed her little brother to dart into the house. As she dropped her backpack in a chair in the foyer she watched him pound up the stairs two at a time. Seconds later the bathroom door slammed shut.

Ellie giggled as she headed to the kitchen for a snack. From the refrigerator she pulled out a brick of cheddar cheese and a jar of gourmet mustard. Then she took two bagels from a plastic bag in the bread box. "Yum," she said aloud, placing two bagel halves in the toaster.

"Ellie!" Hans's panicked voice startled Ellie. She turned away from the toaster.

"What?" she called back, walking out of the kitchen and toward the staircase.

"You've gotta come up here!" Hans's worried face appeared over the railing at the top of the stairs.

"I happen to be in the middle of making us cheddar bagels," Ellie said. But she started up the stairs anyway.

When she reached the second floor, Hans took her hand and pulled her toward the bathroom. "The sink is alive," he explained.

"A sink can't be alive, dummy," Ellie said, shaking her head.

But as soon as she opened the door of the bathroom Ellie's jaw dropped. Water was spewing from the sink faucet in every direction. She held her hand up to her face to guard her eyes from a stream of water. Hans hid behind her, using her as a shield.

"Jeez!" Ellie yelled. She raced toward the faucet. "What did you *do* in here?"

Hans ducked into the shower stall. "Nothing! I swear."

Ellie turned both the hot and cold handles on the faucet, but nothing happened. Water continued to burst out as if the sink had become one of the geysers in Yellowstone Park. "Was the toilet okay?" Ellie yelled over the sound of water.

Hans nodded, looking over at the calm porcelain bowl of the toilet. Ellie followed his gaze, and at that moment the flusher moved of its own accord. A fountain of water sprayed upward, hitting the ceiling.

"Let's get out of here!" Ellie yelled, suddenly terrified. She yanked Hans from the shower and they fell together into the hallway.

Panting, Ellie pulled the bathroom door shut. "I *told* you it was alive," Hans said.

Ellie leaned against the door, breathing rapidly. She had the irrational feeling that she was trapped in a teen horror movie.

From inside the bathroom she could still hear the sound of streams of water hitting the tile. She pressed her ear against the door. "You must have done something to the pipes, Hans."

He shook his head vigorously. "I didn't."

"Water just started spurting everywhere for no reason?"

"Yep."

"Well, I guess I'd better call a plumber," Ellie said, trying to hide the trembling in her voice. "And Mom and Dad." She remembered the mysterious rumbling of the pipes the day before. Had she somehow caused this disaster with her spoiled chemicals?

Ellie took a step away from the door, then stopped. The sound of rushing water was gone. Again she put her ear to the door. This time she heard nothing but a drip, drip, drip.

"Do you think it's over?" Hans asked.

"Only one way to find out." Ellie opened the door slowly and peered inside.

The bathroom looked as if it had been turned upside down. Little streams of water ran down the walls, and there was a big puddle in the middle of the aqua floor. The bath mat and matching towels were sopping wet.

"What a mess!" Hans exclaimed.

Ellie nodded. She'd have to spend the rest of the afternoon putting the bathroom back in order. And trying not to think about the fact that she might have caused the toilet explosion. She picked up the bath mat and towels, holding them at arm's length. "Let's just hope Mom and Dad don't blame us."

"How can they?" Hans asked. "It's not our fault the pipes are alive."

Ellie shook her head at her little brother. "Hans, the pipes are *not,* I repeat, *not* alive."

He shrugged. "That's what you think."

Ellie wished that she could win this argument with Hans. Unfortunately she had the uneasy feeling that for once her little brother was right.

Ellie's stomach lurched. She suspected in her gut that they hadn't heard the last from whatever or *whoever* was inside those pipes. . . .

Chapter

By the time Ellie heard her father's key in the front door at five thirty, she'd managed to get the bathroom to resemble its old self. The puddles were gone, the towels were dry, and she'd used an entire roll of paper towels to soak up the water that had covered the walls. Unfortunately there wasn't much to do about the ceiling.

Now that things were more or less back to normal, she felt stupid for having compared herself to a girl in a horror movie. *I'm a scientist,* she reminded herself. *I* know *that pipes cannot possibly be alive.*

Downstairs, Ellie found Hans holding a plastic bag full of water. Inside the bag two small goldfish swam in circles.

"Replacements," Mr. Volkhausen announced cheerfully.

Hans beamed. "I'm going to name them Spike II and Spike III," he said.

Ellie rolled her eyes. "Those are dumb names."

"Nonsense. I can't think of more fitting names," Mr. Volkhausen said, patting Hans on the shoulder.

"Can we put them in the tank now?" Hans asked.

Mr. Volkhausen loosened his tie as he headed for the stairs. "We'd better. Those little guys might bite us if we don't give them some elbow room."

As they all trooped up the stairs Ellie tried to think of the best way to explain what had happened in the bathroom. But before she could say anything, Hans spoke up.

"Dad, the pipes are alive. Ellie doesn't believe me, but they are."

"What he means is that our house has some big-time plumbing problems," Ellie explained. "I'll show you."

Mr. Volkhausen frowned as he followed them into the bathroom. "I hope you two didn't stop up the toilet with something," he said sternly.

"A stopped-up toilet would be nothing compared to the problem we've got," Ellie said.

Ellie's mouth dropped open as they crowded into the bathroom. The place looked exactly as it had before the plumbing had gone crazy. There was no water dripping from the ceiling, and even the aqua shell-shaped soap in the soap dish was as perfect as it had been before sitting in a pool of water for an hour. Ellie glanced at Hans, but he seemed totally absorbed with Spike II and Spike III.

Slowly Ellie turned the sink faucet. She held her breath, waiting for the water to gush out in every direction.

"I don't see the problem, honey," Mr. Volkhausen said.

Ellie stared at the gleaming silver faucet. There was nothing out of the ordinary about the way the water was running. "I guess the sink fixed itself," she said. "But wait until I flush the toilet."

She reached over and flushed the toilet, keeping her eyes glued to the now calm bowl of water. Again there was nothing strange about the plumbing.

"I'm missing something. Exactly what did you two do to the toilet?" Mr. Volkhausen asked.

Ellie flushed the toilet again, waiting for the water to burst out. What was going on? "Hans, tell Dad what happened earlier."

"There was water *everywhere*. And Ellie couldn't get it to stop." Hans gestured with his bag of fish, waving them around in circles. "It just kept going and going and—"

"I get the point," Mr. Volkhausen interrupted.

"Really, Dad, it was wild," Ellie added.

Mr. Volkhausen raised an eyebrow. "Well, everything seems fine now. Let's forget about water world and do something with those poor fish."

He thinks we're just exaggerating, Ellie realized.

She remembered the way her heart had pounded as water gushed out of every pipe in the bathroom. How could her father not believe them? For the millionth time she cursed being only twelve years old. If she were a grown-up, her dad would *have* to listen to their story.

Now, as she gazed around the picture-perfect bathroom, Ellie promised herself that she would handle the problem on her own.

Not that there necessarily *was* a problem, she reminded herself. Quite possibly it had all been a freak occurrence. Ellie stared at the ceiling and wondered how it had cleaned itself.

"Something's going on here," she said aloud. "If only I knew what it was. . . ."

Chapter

Ellie moved her arms slowly and heavily. They felt different—as if they weren't arms at all. She looked down and realized with a start that she'd grown fins.

"Oh, my gosh," she shouted. Or tried to shout. No words came out.

She studied her surroundings for the first time. Her heart pounded painfully as she saw that she was in a cage. But instead of a square wire cage, it was a glass bowl. A giant fishbowl.

Below her she recognized the same blue, red, and yellow plastic castle that Hans kept in his fish tank. And the bottom of the bowl was covered with the kind of pastel crystals that she always saw at the pet store. Above her head flakes of moldy fish food dotted the water.

Ellie knocked her head against the side of the bowl, looking out. On the other side of the room she saw Hans. He was in a square tank, and a fluorescent light threw strange shadows on his face. Like herself, Hans had lost his arms and legs. In their place were fins and scales. But his blue eyes and dark eyebrows remained, and Ellie wanted to cry as she saw how terrified his expression was.

Suddenly a figure appeared outside her bowl. His beady red eyes seemed as if they would pop out of his head when he sneered at her. He was tall and not quite human. Like Ellie, he had fins and a fish mouth.

Ellie recognized him from her dream the other night. He was back.

"What's going on?" she wondered frantically, ramming again and again into the side of the bowl.

She swam in panicked circles, searching for any way out of her nightmare. But the figure loomed closer and closer. When he was just inches away, Ellie saw that he had a huge net in his fin.

Chapter

After school the next day Ellie leaned her head tiredly against the front door while she groped for her key. She hadn't slept well the night before, and she still felt unsettled from her dream.

"Do you want to help me feed Spike II and Spike III?" Hans asked.

Ellie finally found her key and put it into the lock. "I'm sick of fish," she answered. "Maybe instead of feeding those beasts we should fry them up for an after-school snack."

Hans frowned and pinched her arm hard. "You're mean. I'm going to tell Mom you said that."

"Go ahead," Ellie said, pushing open the front door. "We'll ask her to make some tartar . . ."

Ellie's words died away as she looked around the downstairs. The house looked as if it had been hit by a tornado. Ellie took an involuntary step backward.

"Holy cow!" Hans yelled.

"Stay back, Hans," Ellie ordered. "Whoever did this might still be inside."

From the open door Ellie could see that a chair and small table in the front hall had been knocked over. A bowl where they kept loose change was turned upside down, and dimes, pennies, nickels, and quarters were scattered all over the hardwood floor.

Ellie could also see about half of the living room. Several family photos were on the floor. A framed picture of her grandmother had a long crack down its center.

One large sofa had been shoved halfway across the room, and Ellie saw a dozen slimy footsteps leading away from it. Ellie felt the blood drain from her face.

Everywhere her eyes fell, something was broken or out of place. In the front hall a clay dinosaur that Hans had made in art class lay shattered in a million pieces. Ellie stared at the broken sculpture and shuddered.

Ellie rocked back and forth on her heels, trying

to decide whether or not she should dart inside and call the police. Could a robber be in the kitchen, waiting to get her? She put a hand over her heart, wishing she could make the beating slow to a normal rate.

Hans's voice interrupted her thoughts. "Hi, Andy!" he called. "We've been ramsacked."

"*Ransacked*," Ellie automatically corrected.

Andy stopped his blue ten-speed at the base of the front walk and jogged over to Ellie and Hans.

"What are you talking about?" he asked, his brown eyes warm and serious.

"Take a look," Ellie said. She gestured toward the chaos in the house. "I don't even know if it's safe to go inside."

Andy picked up a large stick and held it above his head. "Follow me," he said in a brave voice. "I'll protect you."

Ellie doubted Andy's ability to protect a flea—he wasn't the most muscular guy around. But she wasn't anxious to go first herself. She hoisted her backpack above her head and followed him into the front hall.

"Hello? Anyone home?" Ellie yelled. The only answer was the loud ticking of the grandfather clock at the bottom of the stairs.

"We're armed and dangerous!" Andy shouted.

33

For a moment the only sound in the house was the beating of their hearts and the sound of water dripping into the kitchen sink.

Andy took a deep breath, then swung open the door of the kitchen and poked his head inside. "Empty," he shouted to Hans and Ellie. "Very messy, but empty."

They started carefully through the house, checking every corner and closet for intruders. First Ellie stuck her head into the pantry and quickly switched on the overhead light. Her heart stopped when she heard a loud crash in the corner.

"Just a can of sliced tomatoes," Andy said from behind her.

Ellie nodded silently and led the way to the family room. Again all was quiet. Ellie pointed to the billowing curtains of the wall-high family room windows, and Andy pulled them back with a flourish.

Specks of dust immediately clouded the air, and Ellie coughed. She shut her eyes for a moment, praying she was safe. When she pried open her eyelids, Andy was staring out the window. There was a film of dust on the hardwood floor.

"No mass murderer here," Andy remarked.

Twenty minutes later Ellie plopped down on an

overstuffed living room sofa. There was no sign of anyone still in the house—and nothing was missing.

"What are all these puddles from?" Hans asked.

Throughout the house there were small, scummy puddles on the floor. When she'd bent close to one, Ellie had inhaled the nauseating scent of spoiled fish. The odor had reminded her of the time their deep freezer had gone out and twenty pounds of trout had sat rotting in the basement for three days.

Now Ellie thought of the plumbing disaster the day before and felt a chill. The idea that the two events were connected was totally crazy, but still . . .

Finally Andy and Ellie crept into Mr. and Mrs. Volkhausen's bedroom. The king-size bed was still perfectly made, and not one item was out of place. "Whoever was in the house obviously didn't want anything in here," Andy said, looking around.

Ellie nodded thoughtfully. The room seemed almost too peaceful, *too* silent. The hairs on the back of her neck stood up as she made her way slowly to the bathroom off the master bedroom.

Just outside the door Ellie stopped and listened. Her heart pounded as she heard the distinct sound of running water. "Mom? Dad?" she called.

The water stopped, but there was no response. Ellie motioned Andy forward with her hand. He tiptoed to the door, holding the stick as if it were a baseball bat. Ellie reached over to her mom's nightstand and picked up a large brass paperweight.

"One, two . . ." Ellie whispered. She looked at Andy, and he put his hand on the doorknob of the bathroom. "Three!"

Andy flung open the door, and Ellie rushed into the bathroom.

"Aaaaa . . . aaaa!" she screamed.

In the middle of the bathroom, standing in a puddle of water, was the most hideous creature Ellie had ever seen. The thing was tall and thin, a long column of solid muscle. His skin was the color of pond algae and covered with thick, flaky scales. Something that looked like mucus dripped from his body to the floor. At the top of his body was a small head with a huge, sharp-toothed jaw. Worst of all, the monster had glowing red eyes set deeply into his pointed skull.

Spike, she thought in disbelief.

There was no doubt about it. The *thing* that ogled at her through shining eyes looked exactly like Hans's dead fish, Spike. Only bigger—much bigger.

"It's not human," Andy whispered hoarsely. The stick fell uselessly to his side.

"Who are you?" Ellie shouted.

The creature groaned in response, then made its way forward on legs that looked like overgrown fish fins.

Ellie felt Hans come up behind her. He clutched the back of her shirt, and she could tell that her brother was trembling with fright. So was she.

"It's Spike," Hans said. He hid his face against Ellie's back.

Ellie was paralyzed with fear. Next to her Andy stood with his mouth open.

Suddenly the creature let out a horrible shriek. Green slime oozed from its puckered mouth and dribbled to the floor. Ellie felt the touch of the monster's rough scales. *I'm going to die,* Ellie screamed silently. *We're all going to die.*

Chapter

Ellie squeezed her eyes shut. "This isn't happening. This is a nightmare. This isn't happening."

She said the words over and over, hoping against hope that the cold grip of the fish creature would disappear. But when she opened her eyes again, he was still there, staring at her through those same cold fish eyes.

"Watch out, El!" Hans suddenly yelled.

Hans hurled a thick, hardback book through the air. It hit the monster squarely between the eyes. As swiftly as the creature had put his steel grip on Ellie's arm, he now let go.

Her legs shaking, Ellie watched in amazement as the monster stretched himself as thin and long as a giant snake. His greenish body looked like a menacing garden hose, and his red eyes appeared even larger.

Ellie gasped as the creature poured himself into the round drain of Mr. and Mrs. Volkhausen's sink. His entire body disappeared into the maze of pipes behind the walls.

Ellie sank to her knees and took a moment to catch her breath. "Tell me that was all in my imagination," she said to Andy.

He shook his head. "I wish I could. Believe me."

Hans jumped up and down. "Spike is alive!"

Ellie managed to stand up, although her legs still felt like spaghetti. "Let's discuss this in the kitchen," she said.

Downstairs, Ellie moved around the kitchen like a robot. She stuck a bagel in the toaster, trying to block from her mind the image of the fish creature.

"How can you eat at a time like this?" Andy asked.

Ellie put a hand over the growing lump in her stomach. "I can't. But I'm hoping that making a snack will calm me down."

"I can eat," Hans announced, glancing at the toaster.

"Does either of you have any idea what that . . . *thing* was?" Andy asked, looking from Ellie to Hans.

Hans stuffed a handful of pretzels into his mouth. "Ellie brought Spike back to life with one of her experiments."

Ellie grabbed the two bagel halves as they popped up. She'd had exactly the same thought as soon as she'd seen Spike's new, deformed body. There was no other answer.

"As crazy as that sounds, he must be right," she said to Andy.

"But, Ellie, that's impossible," Andy said.

Ellie glared at her best friend. "Do you doubt my scientific ability?" she asked.

Andy shrugged as he reached for the bag of pretzels. "*Of course* I doubt your ability to create a monster who lives in your pipes. It's impossible."

"But we *saw* it," Hans pointed out.

Ellie sat down, pondering the events of the last couple of days.

"Remember when I flushed those chemicals the other night?" she asked Hans.

"Yeah! The water turned all purple and fizzy," he answered.

She turned to Andy. "It was the experiment you were helping me with—or a variation of it.

After dinner the chemicals were a mess, so I got rid of them."

"And your experiment met up with Spike," Andy concluded softly. "Somehow, some way, the mixture changed Spike into the creature that we saw upstairs."

Ellie's stomach churned. "I created a monster."

"Spike wouldn't hurt anybody," Hans said loudly.

"Yes, Hans, he would," Ellie said, her voice serious. "If you hadn't been smart enough to hit him with Mom's book, he might have killed all of us."

"At least he's gone," Andy said. He sighed heavily as he scraped the salt off a pretzel.

"For now." Fear traveled up Ellie's spine as she wondered when Spike would make another appearance.

"Is Spike really bad?" Hans asked.

Andy patted Hans on the back. "'Fraid so, buddy. He's not the same fish who was your pet."

"We probably just scared him," Hans insisted. "I'm sure he's still as awesome as Spike always was."

Ellie thought back to Spike's small, glowing eyes. Then she remembered the long, sharp teeth that jutted from between his gray-black lips. She shook her head. "He's evil."

41

Hans's bottom lip trembled. "Is Dad going to have to kill him?"

Ellie sat up straight in her chair. For the last hour she'd completely forgotten that her parents even existed. "Oh, my gosh. What are we going to tell Mom and Dad?"

"Well, you can't tell them the truth," Andy said. "They wouldn't believe you in a million years."

"Why not?" Hans asked.

Ellie glanced around the messy kitchen. How could she explain to Hans that grown-ups were incapable of accepting any notion that seemed out of the ordinary? "Just trust us, Hans. Andy and I will have to deal with Spike on our own."

"I wanna tell Mom and Dad," Hans insisted.

Ellie rubbed her temples, which had started to ache. "We're not telling them anything. They'll just make things worse."

Andy crunched another pretzel. "Listen, buddy, if you keep our secret, Ellie and I will let you help us deal with Spike."

Hans seemed to brighten. "Really?"

Ellie glared at Andy, but he just smiled calmly at her. "Really," Andy promised. "You can be an official fish-monster buster."

"All right!" Hans shouted.

Ellie sighed. Andy had sealed their fate. Now

she not only had to worry about a murderous fish in the pipes—she also had to keep an eye on her pesky little brother. "Before anybody does anything, we've got to get this place cleaned up," she said.

Andy and Hans groaned. "Do we have to?" Hans asked.

Ellie stood up. "Get moving," she said loudly. "Now!"

As she spoke a loud banging came from the pipes buried deep beneath the house. Ellie's heart leapt in her throat and she jumped, knocking over a kitchen chair. She had to come up with a plan to get rid of this monster—and there wasn't a moment to waste.

Chapter

At six o'clock Ellie slid the lasagna her mother had left in the freezer into the oven. "I'm exhausted."

Ellie leaned heavily against the counter, shutting her eyes for a moment. Her muscles ached from cleaning and moving furniture—and she and Andy hadn't come any closer to a monster solution.

"Ellie, come check this out." Andy was sitting at the kitchen table. In front of him the yellow pages were open to PLUMBERS.

Hans looked up from his peanut butter on toast. "Can I see?"

"Sure, bud."

Ellie and Hans took a seat on either side of Andy. "What did you find?" Ellie asked. She felt hopeful for the first time all afternoon.

"Look for yourself," Andy said. He pushed the yellow pages forward, and Ellie saw that he'd circled one ad with blue pen.

Ellie read the lines of the advertisement quickly, her heart racing.

EVERYTHING PLUMBING
Larry Lobo will clean your pipes
no matter WHAT is stopping them up.
We specialize in monsters, ghosts, and
other creatures of the supernatural sort.
Call now: 555–3293

"Do you think this guy is for real?" Ellie asked.

Andy pushed his glasses up on his nose, then studied the ad again. "Only one way to find out," he said finally.

Ellie glanced at her watch. "We've only got a half hour before my mom gets home."

"So make an appointment for tomorrow," Andy suggested.

Ellie bit her lip. "How will we pay him?"

"We'll worry about the bill later. Right now the monster has to be the first priority."

"You're right," Ellie said. She went to the baby

blue wall phone, lugging the phone book with her.

"Can I call?" Hans asked.

"No way," Ellie said. "This is important." She dialed the number of Larry Lobo, mentally willing him to be in his office.

After four rings she heard a man's low voice. "Yallo?" he said.

"Uh, is this Mr. Lobo?" Ellie asked.

"Sure is. What can I do fer ya?"

Ellie cleared her throat to stall for time. "Tell him!" Andy hissed.

Ellie covered the phone's mouthpiece with her hand. "Explaining the fact that you've created a monster in your toilet isn't the easiest thing in the world to do," she whispered back.

"Yallo! Anybody there?" Larry Lobo's loud voice boomed in Ellie's ear.

"Yes, Mr. Lobo, I'm here. Uh, my name is Ellie Volkhausen, and, uh, I have a problem with the pipes in our house."

"Call me Larry. All my friends do."

"Okay . . . Larry. Like I was saying, my little brother and I have a problem."

On the other end of the line Larry Lobo chuckled. "What is it? Ghost? Monster? Unidentified creature?"

"We think it's a monster," Ellie said. She couldn't believe that Larry didn't sound at all surprised.

"What variety of monster is it?" Larry asked. Ellie heard something fall with a thump to the floor. Larry chuckled again.

"It's my brother's fish. Sort of." Ellie remembered the horrible sight of Spike. She didn't think a description could do the creature justice.

"Not to worry, Ellie. Fish monsters are my specialty."

"Great, Mr. Lobo . . . Larry. I'm really glad to hear that."

"Now, when can we set up an appointment?"

Ellie glanced at Andy and Hans, who were staring at her with rapt attention. "Tomorrow afternoon?"

"Let me just check my schedule," Larry answered.

Ellie heard him leaf through the pages of his calendar. Could there really be other people who needed his services? Maybe the sewers were filled with monsters, and she'd never known about it. Ellie shuddered at the thought of a whole pack of Spikes.

"Lucky for you business is slow," Larry finally said. "I'm free all afternoon."

"Thank you, Mr. Lobo. We really appreciate it." Ellie already felt relieved. The plumber didn't sound concerned—he even seemed to be looking forward to their meeting.

"What's yer address?" he asked.

"Five-three-two-two Sunset Drive."

"Okay, then. I'll need you to gather some items for us to use. Can you do that?"

Ellie took a pen and pad to write down the list. "Of course. Anything to help."

"Okey-dokey. Rubber gloves. A few flashlights. A hard hat for yourself and anyone involved. Rubber boots. And nose plugs."

"Yes, sir," Ellie responded. As she wrote she tried to imagine what the plumber planned to do with all the items. She felt her throat tighten.

"See you tomorrow, Ellie," Larry said. "And be prepared to get 'im!"

Ellie hung up the phone, mulling over Larry Lobo's final words. The plumber obviously expected them to be on hand to help him fight the monster.

Ellie pressed her lips tightly together, already dreading what would surely be the scariest afternoon of her life. Even worse, if Larry Lobo's plan didn't succeed, the next afternoon could also be her *last*.

Chapter

11

"I'm worried about having you-know-who with us this afternoon," Andy said to Ellie on Wednesday afternoon.

Ellie popped open a can of soda, contemplating Hans. "I'm torn about it," she admitted. "On the one hand, I don't want him blabbing to his little friends that we're searching for a monster."

"On the other hand, you don't want him to totally freak out," Andy finished.

Ellie nodded. "You got it."

"I guess we'll just have to wait for Larry Lobo to get here and see what happens." Andy propped his feet up on the Volkhausens' kitchen table. "I just hope he arrives *soon*."

Ellie downed the rest of her soda in three gulps. She was always extra thirsty when she was nervous, and today was no exception. "At least Spike hasn't shown up again."

"Yet." Andy stood up and paced the length of the kitchen.

Ellie gritted her teeth. Andy's impatience was catching. "Andy, you're driving me crazy. Can you just sit down?"

He paused at the corner of the kitchen table and raised an eyebrow. "I'll check on Hans. He's probably trying to convince Spike II and Spike III that he's not some kind of fish hater."

"Good idea. I'll wait for Larry Lobo." Ellie grabbed another soda from the fridge as she listened to Andy clomp up the stairs.

Only thirty seconds later Ellie heard three quick beeps from a car horn. "Larry Lobo!" she said aloud. "Thank goodness."

She jogged to the foyer and swung open the front door. Ellie didn't know exactly what she'd been expecting the plumber to look like, but the sight of Larry Lobo made her jaw drop.

He was striding up the Volkhausens' brick walkway, whistling a strange tune that Ellie didn't recognize. "Hi there!" he yelled, waving cheerfully.

Ellie swallowed hard. "Uh, hi, Mr. Lobo," she called. "I'm happy to see you." *I think,* she added to herself.

Andy appeared suddenly at Ellie's side. "Yikes!" he whispered. "What have we gotten ourselves into?"

She almost giggled as she watched the plumber continue toward them. Larry Lobo was wearing a neon purple jumpsuit, an orange baseball cap, and bright red high-top tennis shoes. He wore thick glasses that looked as if they'd been through World War III. Around his waist was a wide leather belt, which emphasized his fat, bouncing stomach. Various tools hung from the belt, all banging against his sides as he walked.

"Well, now," he said when he reached the front door. "You must be Ellie."

"Yes, sir." Ellie shook his big hand.

"And who's this feller?" Larry Lobo asked, smiling at Andy.

"I'm Andy Stein, Mr. Lobo. A friend of Ellie's."

As Larry Lobo shook Andy's hand Hans poked his head out the door. "I'm Hans," he announced.

"Nice ta meet ya, Hansie," the plumber responded. "And y'all call me Larry. Bein' called 'Mr.' makes me feel like an old man."

Ellie led the group into the kitchen, where she gave Larry a brief rundown of how she'd accidentally created Spike and what had happened since. Larry nodded as she spoke but said nothing.

When she was done, he winked.

"Well, now, we've got quite a project on our hands. Yes, siree, *quite* a project. Can't say that I've had this kind of challenge in *quite* some time."

Ellie's spirits sank. As far as she could tell, Larry Lobo didn't have any easy answers. In fact, she wasn't sure he had any answers at all. "So what should we *do,* Larry?"

The plumber folded his hands over his large stomach and grinned at them all. "Do you have the equipment I told you to get?"

Andy pointed to a pile on the counter. "Right over there, Larry."

"Wonderful, wonderful," he boomed. "Now, there's only one problem."

"What's that?" Ellie asked. She'd already moved to the pile of flashlights, hats, and rubber boots.

"Hansie here might be a little young for our adventure." He paused. "We're going underground."

"Underground?" Ellie asked, her voice little more than a squeak.

"Yup. Right into the guts of this town."

Andy squinted at Larry through the thick lenses of his glasses. "What do you mean by 'guts'?"

Larry cracked each of his knuckles, drawing out the suspense of the moment. "I *mean* we're going to go down into the sewer system."

"What?" Ellie yelped. The idea of walking through dark tunnels full of raw sewage made her gag.

"We've got to catch this monster where he lives. It's our best bet for *total extermination*."

"Total extermination," Ellie echoed quietly.

"This isn't going to be pretty, is it?" Andy asked Larry.

The plumber wiggled his dark, bushy, eyebrows. "If everything goes according to plan, the afternoon could turn very, very ugly."

Larry Lobo turned his head . . . and smashed his glasses right into an open kitchen cabinet. Ellie's heart sank as she saw the lenses pop out and fall to the ground. She bent to pick them up, but Larry took a step, accidentally grinding one lens under the heel of his work boot.

Ellie shot a look at Andy. "He's a fool," Andy mouthed.

Ellie nodded, fresh fear rising up inside her. She'd already guessed that Larry was pretty stupid—now he was blind as well. Which meant killing the monster was entirely up to her.

Ellie put a protective arm around Hans's shoulders. Was her little brother really prepared for blood, guts, and raw sewage? For that matter, was she?

Chapter

"Do you think Hans will be all right?" Ellie asked anxiously.

Andy swung his flashlight over his shoulder and adjusted the wide rim of his plastic toy fireman's hat. "He's a smart kid, El. He'll be fine."

"Mom and Dad would kill me if they knew I left him home alone."

"We told him not to answer the door, not to leave, and not to touch anything that could possibly get hot. What else is there?"

Ellie sighed heavily. "I just hope he doesn't get scared and freak out. I locked all the bathrooms."

Larry stopped in front of a manhole about halfway down the block. Ellie still had a full view of the Volkhausens' house, which made her feel a little better.

"Prepare to go *down!*" Larry said. He punched the air with his fist.

Andy gave Larry a high five. "Cool! I've never been under the streets before."

Ellie wrinkled her nose. "Aren't there rats and all sorts of dead stuff down there?"

"We're on a mission," Larry reminded her. "We can't worry about unimportant things like rats."

Ellie took a deep breath. *I can do this,* she told herself. "Lead the way, Larry," she said finally.

Larry grinned as he lifted the heavy lid that covered the manhole. He set the metal disk aside, then knelt on the street. "It's a tight fit for me—but I'll squeeze through if it kills me."

Ellie adjusted her bright yellow plastic hard hat as she watched Larry struggle to lower himself into the sewer. "Do you really think he can do it?" she whispered to Andy.

"I hope so," Andy replied, a skeptical expression on his face.

Larry disappeared from sight. "Come on down," he called from beneath the street. "There's plenty of room."

"Go ahead, El," Andy said. He gave her a soft push toward the gaping hole.

Ellie tucked her flashlight into the waistband of her jeans. Then she sat down at the edge of the hole, allowing her legs to dangle over the edge. Finally she took a deep breath and jumped.

Ellie landed easily and found herself right next to Larry Lobo. He had turned on his powerful flashlight and was scanning the interior of the sewer system with its bright beam.

Andy's face appeared above the manhole. "Move out of the way, Ellie. I'm coming down."

Ellie scooted quickly toward the slime-covered wall. A second later Andy was beside her. "Wow, this place is intense," he said softly.

Ellie nodded as she turned on her own flashlight. The underground was like a whole other world. Concrete paths seemed to lead in every direction, and the air was damp and heavy. A small stream trickled under her feet, making her glad that she'd followed Larry's advice and worn rubber boots. A smell like rotting old food wafted through the tunnels.

"How are we going to find our way around?" Ellie asked anxiously.

Larry held up a piece of paper. "Simple. I've got a map of the entire system. I got it years ago when I worked for the Sanitation Department."

Andy trained his beam over Larry's shoulder

and moved closer so that he could see the map. "Where are we headed?"

Ellie inched close to Andy and stared at the spot on the map that Larry pointed to. "I figure around here's our best bet," Larry explained, circling the spot with his finger. "There'd be plenty of room for a monster's lair."

"Lead the way," Andy said.

Larry folded the map and stuffed it into a pouch hanging off the side of his tool belt. He shined his flashlight down a tunnel, lighting a few feet of the dark path. "Y'all turn off your lights. No sense wastin' batteries."

Larry started down the path. Andy followed, and Ellie brought up the rear. As she walked, Ellie concentrated only on the light of Larry's flashlight and the sound of his cheerful whistling. With every step she tried to block out thoughts of both Hans at home and the monster who waited for them.

Soon they were deep in the maze of the underground sewers. Ellie tried not to gag as the stench grew stronger. *Be brave,* she told herself.

"I feel like an ancient explorer," Andy commented, breaking the tension. "We're conquering new territory."

"Ah, a boy after my own heart," Larry responded. "Nothing is so satisfying as—"

Larry's voice broke off, and Ellie skidded to a stop. The tunnel was suddenly plunged into darkness. She heard Andy gasp and a groan from Larry Lobo.

"What happened?" she whispered in a trembling voice.

Before either of her companions could respond, Ellie felt a cold, wet hand clutch her shoulder. Gripped with terror, Ellie opened her mouth and let out a piercing scream that echoed through the pitch-black tunnel. . . .

Chapter

"Ellie!" Andy shouted in her ear. "Shut up!"

Ellie felt the cold, wet hand shake her shoulder roughly. The sound of her screams seemed to be coming from another person. She was powerless to stop the horrible noise. "*Aaaaaa!*"

"Everything's fine, El. Just calm down." Again Andy's voice broke through the roar in Ellie's ears.

The tight grip on her shoulder relaxed. As the same hand patted her soothingly on the back she realized that the hand belonged to Andy—not some creature of the dark. The screaming stopped abruptly and she sighed deeply. "Don't *do* that!" she snapped.

"Don't do what?" Andy asked. He turned on his flashlight and held the beam toward her face.

"Scare me!" Ellie shouted.

"Sorreee . . ." Andy took several steps away from her.

Turning on her own flashlight, Ellie pointed the beam in Larry's general direction. For the first time since they'd been without light, Ellie realized that Larry had slipped and fallen.

"Minor setback, kids. Nothin' to get rattled about," Larry called in his booming voice.

Andy helped Larry to his feet, and the plumber turned his light back on. "Be careful, El," Andy said. "There's some major slime over here."

Ellie forced a shaky laugh. "I definitely don't want to fall down in the stuff—whatever it is."

"Onward!" Larry's deep voice echoed off the walls of the tunnel, making Ellie feel as if she were standing at the bottom of a gigantic canyon.

They shuffled forward at a slower pace, moving deeper and deeper into the maze. After several silent minutes they emerged from the tunnel into a larger cavern.

"What is this place?" Ellie asked. Now that her eyes had adjusted to the darkness, she could make out the gray shadows of the large objects that lined the walls of the room.

"Sort of a second town dump," Larry said. He flashed his light on a broken toilet, a rotting Laz-E-Boy, a baby crib, and what looked like an old-fashioned pizza oven.

"Jeez! Look at all this junk," Andy exclaimed. "How does it get down here?"

Larry shrugged. "One a' life's mysteries, buddy."

"Can we get on with this hunt?" Ellie demanded. "Hans is still alone in the house."

"Got the creeps?" Larry asked.

"Big time," Ellie admitted. She shuddered as she noticed a coffin-shaped box in the corner.

"We're real close now," Larry said. He crossed the room and stood at the entrance of yet another tunnel.

The new passage was smaller than the last. Ellie reached up and touched the damp, slimy ceiling. Past the tips of her fingers there was only a couple of feet of space. "I hope this tunnel doesn't get any smaller," she whispered to Andy.

"No kidding. Larry could get stuck!" he whispered back.

Their footsteps echoed against the concrete floor as they continued toward the center of town. After another hundred yards the feel of the air changed again. A foul odor that Ellie couldn't identify as anything she'd ever smelled before filled the passage. Ellie coughed, then covered her mouth and nose with her hand.

"Aha!" Larry exclaimed. "He's close."

"How do you know?" Andy asked. He'd plugged his nose, and his voice sounded strange and high pitched.

"I can smell 'im," Larry said proudly. "Can't you?"

"Most definitely," Ellie replied. She squeezed her own nostrils tightly together and applied her nose plug.

Larry stopped quickly. Andy and Ellie huddled behind his wide back and peered over his shoulder. "I think this is it. The monster's lair," the plumber said quietly. "He's gotta be here somewhere."

They were staring into another room, much smaller than the last. Ellie could see shadows and forms, but no movement. An electric shiver of fear traveled up her spine.

"Exactly what are we going to do when we find him?" Ellie asked, keeping her voice low.

"Well, uh, we're going to, ah, teach 'im a thing or two," Larry answered.

"Like what?" Andy asked.

"Er, uh, not to mess with this group." Larry took a red bandanna out of his pocket and mopped the sweat off his forehead.

"*How* are we going to manage that?" Ellie asked, feeling panic rise within her. She was getting the distinct sense that Larry Lobo had no idea what he was doing.

"Y'all just wait and see," Larry responded. "Now come on."

They edged slowly into the cave, keeping close to the wall. Larry shined his beam across the floor, revealing a dark, slimy pit of water in the center of the room.

"Yuck!" Ellie could imagine herself falling deep into the pool of water, sinking like a stone to its bottom.

Andy whistled softly. "Do you think he's in there?" he asked Larry.

Ellie held her breath as Larry walked toward the pool. As the beam of his flashlight moved across the water, Ellie saw that the surface was completely still.

"Maybe we're in the wrong place," she suggested.

"I don't think so," Andy said. He flashed his light to a patch of concrete near the edge of the pool.

Ellie's heart dropped to her feet as she saw Hans's Kermit the Frog beach towel lying in a muddy heap. "Oh."

"The monster must have been in your house

while you guys were at school and brought back a souvenir," Andy said.

"Oh," Ellie repeated. The thought of Spike prowling through their empty house made her blood run cold. How many times had he been there?

"Well, he ain't here now." Larry sounded both disappointed and relieved.

"If he's not here, then where is he?" Ellie wondered aloud.

"He's probably out terrorizin' somebody," Larry said.

Suddenly Ellie reached out and clutched Andy's sleeve. A vision of Hans alone in the house flashed through her mind. "Hans!" she shouted.

Andy's eyes widened. "We've got to get back," he said, already turning toward the entrance of the cave.

"What's that?" Larry asked, still staring into the pool.

"My brother!" Ellie screamed. "He could get killed!"

She beat Andy to the tunnel opening and started to run. Blindly she felt her way along the dark path. Every second counted.

I'm coming, Hans, she shouted silently. *Please hang on until I get there.*

Chapter

Ellie dug her house key out of her front pocket as she raced up the front path. She was panting, and her lungs felt as if they were close to bursting. Andy was close behind, holding his side and breathing heavily. Larry Lobo was still halfway down the block, walking at a leisurely pace.

After what seemed like forever, Ellie managed to turn the key in the lock. "Hans," she shouted. "Where are you?"

When there was no answer, Ellie headed up the stairs two at a time. "Hans, we're home!"

"I'll look in the kitchen," Andy called.

Tears blinded Ellie's eyes as she reached the top of the staircase. The house was deadly quiet, just as Spike's lair had been.

Even as she pushed open the door of Hans's room, she knew he wouldn't be inside. Looking in, Ellie saw the usual piles of toys and clothes on the floor. A half-eaten peanut butter and jelly sandwich was on a plate on his bed. In the middle of the room Hans had started a finger painting on a large piece of paper. But he was nowhere in sight.

"He's not down here," Andy yelled upstairs.

Ellie's stomach tightened into a painful lump. She leaned against the door of Hans's room, unable to decide what to do next.

A second later Ellie heard the sound of running water. She pushed herself away from the doorjamb and ran down the hall. Ellie half expected the door to be locked—or blocked by something—but the knob turned easily.

Ellie looked into the bathroom and her eyes almost popped out of her head. Hans was inside the shower stall, which was rapidly filling with water. His head was near the top of the shower, and he was gasping for air. Ellie could see that he was exhausted from treading water—his wet clothes and sneakers probably added several pounds to his body weight. Hans was trapped in a human fishbowl.

"Hans!" she screamed, leaping toward the shower door. "What's going on?"

"Help me!" he yelled, his voice desperate.

The long silver bar of the towel rack had been ripped from the wall and stuck in the door of the shower, locking Hans inside. Gobs of the black slime that covered Spike's body lay in puddles all over the floor.

"I'll get you out!" Ellie yelled. "Stay calm."

She pulled the towel rack from the handle and threw it aside. As the metal bar clattered against the green tiles of the bathroom floor Ellie yanked open the shower door.

Water rushed out, immediately flooding the bathroom floor. Ellie reached into the shower and gripped her brother's arms. She dragged him into the bathroom, then picked him up and set him on top of the sink. Hans folded his knees and hugged them with his arms. Tears streamed down his pale face.

"Are you okay?" Ellie asked.

He nodded but continued to cry with deep, shuddering breaths. "Spike was here," Hans explained between sobs.

"I figured that," Ellie said. Now that she knew Hans was safe, she turned back to the shower.

Both the hot and cold taps were going full blast. Ellie turned and turned the knobs, but water continued to pour from the showerhead. "It won't turn off," she called to Hans.

Andy appeared at the door of the bathroom. "Can I help?"

"Get a wrench. There's one under the kitchen sink." She pushed her drenched bangs out of her eyes and continued to twist the knobs in vain. Even though Ellie wasn't actually trapped in the shower, she began to understand just how terrified Hans must have been.

"Here, Ellie." Andy handed her the wrench.

She tightened the steel jaws of the wrench around first one tap and then the other. Finally the water stopped, and Ellie breathed a sigh of relief. For the moment the crisis was over.

"What happened, Hans?" Andy asked.

Ellie handed her brother a dry towel while they waited for his response. Hans's voice was muffled as he rubbed his sopping wet hair.

"I was in my room painting, and I got blue all over my hands." His face appeared from behind the towel and he pointed at a trace of blue paint in the sink. "So I came in here to wash my hands."

"I told you not to," Ellie said.

"Let me guess," Andy interrupted. "Spike was waiting for you."

"Yeah. But I didn't see him right away."

Fresh tears came to Ellie's eyes as she thought of how scared Hans must have been. She couldn't believe how quickly he'd stopped his tears. By now he was almost cheerful. "Why didn't you see him?" she asked.

"He was behind the door."

"Oh, yeah. There's some slime back here," Andy said, studying the back of the bathroom door.

"Right when I was washing my hands, he popped out," Hans continued.

"Jeez. If the monster jumped out at me, I'd probably have a heart attack," Ellie said.

Andy nodded. "Me too. You're brave, bud."

"Thanks." Hans flexed one of his nonexistent muscles and grinned at them.

"So how did you end up in the shower?"

Hans's face darkened. "He started coming at me. I kept backing up, trying to stay away from him."

"And?" Ellie prompted.

"He locked me in the shower and somehow turned on the water." Hans clutched his towel close to his chest as if it were a teddy bear.

In her mind Ellie saw the muddy Kermit the Frog towel that Spike had taken to his lair. She had no doubt that Spike could have killed Hans on the spot if he'd wanted to. So why hadn't he?

"He's toying with us," Ellie said suddenly.

"Spike's going to keep up with this torture until he gets bored." She paused. "And then he'll murder us, one by one."

Chapter

15

After school the next day Ellie turned to Andy. "I'm at a total loss," she said with a sigh. Her feet had felt like lumps of clay as she'd dragged them toward home, and now her stomach was a one big knot.

"Me too," Andy said through a mouthful of grilled cheese sandwich.

"Me three," Hans declared.

Ellie picked up Hans's plate and moved to the kitchen sink. The familiar house felt like a giant death trap, and Ellie had absolutely no idea how to escape.

"Larry Lobo is just a crazy old man. He was *less* than no help." Ellie's voice held a mixture of fear and frustration.

Andy nodded. "Yeah. He's nice, but I don't think he's going to solve the Spike situation."

"Maybe Spike won't bother us anymore," Hans said hopefully. "Maybe he swam to the ocean."

"I wish that were true," Ellie answered. "But I doubt it."

"Well, he's not here now," Andy pointed out.

Ellie hoisted herself on top of the kitchen counter, then gazed thoughtfully out the window. "If he's gone for good, wonderful."

Suddenly the water in the sink turned on. Ellie jumped from the counter, staring at the heavy stream of water.

"That was you," Andy said. "Your elbow hit the tap."

Ellie sighed with relief. "Like I said, if he's gone for good, wonderful."

"But if he's not . . ." Andy prompted.

"If he's not, we've got to be ready." Ellie opened a drawer under the counter.

She pulled out a blank legal pad and a black felt tip marker, then plunked down next to Hans at the table. On the top of the first sheet of paper she wrote IDEAS.

"Okay. Who's got the first idea?" she asked.

They all jumped from their chairs as a loud banging sounded from inside the den. Ellie ran to the open door of the den and looked in, her heart pounding wildly. Again she sighed with relief. "Just a window closing in the wind," she called.

Moments later she was back in her seat. "Okay, ideas." Silence. They all stared at one another, waiting for someone to speak. Thirty seconds passed. Then a minute. Finally Hans opened his mouth. "Can I have another peanut butter sandwich?" he asked.

Ellie put the cap back on her pen and stood up. "I'm going to go for a swim. Maybe the exercise will clear my head. I'm too jumpy to think clearly right now."

"I'll get Hans another sandwich," Andy offered. "We'll come outside in a few minutes."

Ellie ran upstairs and put on her favorite beat-up navy tank suit. Her room was quiet and peaceful. For a moment Ellie let herself pretend that the monster didn't exist. But when she left her room, she caught sight of the bathroom door.

Slowly she approached the room where she'd seen Hans trapped in a human fishbowl less than twenty-four hours ago. Ellie threw open the door. But the bathroom was empty. Breathing a sigh of relief, Ellie tightly closed the door behind her.

Outside, the sun was shining brightly. Ellie set her beach towel next to the pool ladder, then dove headfirst into the deep end. The cold water was shocking, but she forced herself to sink all the way to the bottom of the pool. After a few seconds she kicked her way to the surface, already longing for a breath of fresh air.

Ellie hung on to the side of the pool, gulping huge breaths. Finally her body became used to the temperature of the water, and she turned to start a set of laps.

She sliced through the water, kicking her legs and pumping her arms as hard as she could. As she swam Ellie blocked out the image of Spike. Slowly her mind relaxed and she began to enjoy the rhythm of her exercise. For the first time in days she felt completely safe—the pool was like another world.

Ellie slapped the edge of the deep end with one hand and did her best kick turn. With her foot she pushed hard against the wall, gaining speed for her next lap. But as she reached forward with her right arm she suddenly felt something hard and cold grab it.

Spike, she screamed in her mind. *The pool drain!* Struggling against the weight of his pull, she cursed herself for having been so stupid. How could she not have realized that Spike could slide through *any* drain, not just the ones in the bathrooms?

Ellie felt the sting of chlorine as her eyes flew open and she stared at the monster. His face was just inches from hers, and his jaws snapped open and closed over and over again. Ellie's muscles ached as she tried to get away. Her heart beat crazily inside her chest, and she knew that within seconds she would drown.

Suddenly a dark movement, which Ellie recognized as a stray leaf at the other end of the pool, caught Spike's attention. When he turned to look, Ellie braced her feet against his slimy body and pushed with all her strength.

Her hand slipped out of the monster's grasp, and she began rapidly scissor kicking her legs. Spike reached out to grab her ankle, but Ellie managed to escape his hold.

In the next moment her head was miraculously above water. "Andy!" she cried weakly, praying that her friend would hear. "Hans!"

Before she could yell again, the monster wrapped his tentaclelike fins around her shin. He sucked Ellie underwater, her arms and legs thrashing. The sounds of the outside world were drowned out and Spike's long, thin body seemed to take up the entire pool.

Panic surged through Ellie's veins as Spike's grip became tighter and tighter. She wanted to fight him, but her energy was almost gone. She felt herself slipping out of consciousness.

Unless a miracle happened, Ellie was sure she'd taken her last breath.

Chapter

With the last of her strength Ellie forced open her eyes. Instantly she regretted the decision. Spike's fireball eyes bored dangerously into hers. Ellie craned her neck away from his head, positive that any second now his eyes would actually shoot sparks.

Ellie went limp, letting her arms and legs dangle uselessly in his grip. *Maybe he'll think I'm dead and let me go,* she told herself. Then a terrifying thought occurred to her. *Maybe I am dead.*

But as the monster's arm tightened even more painfully, Ellie realized that she was very much alive. And completely at his mercy.

For what seemed like hours Ellie had been resisting the urge to let out her breath. At last, with Spike's fins biting into her flesh, she lost the will to fight any longer.

Air whooshed out of Ellie's lungs, sending bubbles to the surface of the pool. She choked as water filled her mouth and nose. Immediately Spike eased his grip. *This is it,* she thought. *He knows he's won.* She was going to die. She'd never win the Nobel Prize. She'd never even graduate from junior high. Her life was over.

As thought after thought raced through Ellie's mind, she saw a large silver pole appear near her side. At its end was a square mesh net. With a surge of hope she recognized the pool strainer. The piece of equipment couldn't have gotten into the pool on its own. Someone outside must be guiding it.

Seeing that the strainer was outside Spike's immediate field of vision, Ellie grabbed for it with her free right hand. Surprised by the sudden movement, the monster let go of her arm.

That second was all the time Ellie needed. Her fingers closed around the steel pole as if her life depended on her ability to make a fist. *My life does depend on this,* she reminded herself.

Before Ellie knew what was happening, she felt the pole being jerked upward. Spike lunged forward, his red eyes burning with rage.

But he was too late. Ellie's head reached the surface of the water. She burst into the air, taking a huge breath. Nothing had ever felt so good.

"Ellie, are you all right?" Andy shouted.

Ellie just shook her head, unable to speak. Both Andy and Hans were holding on to the long handle of the strainer. They continued to pull her toward the wall of the pool as fast as they could.

Beneath the water Spike's long body moved swiftly. "Hurry!" Ellie managed to scream.

Andy and Hans gave the strainer one last hard yank. Ellie felt herself hurtling over the side of the pool. She landed on the soft grass of the Volkhausens' back lawn, coughing and choking.

The sudden absence of her weight on the steel pole caused Hans and Andy to fly backward. They landed on their butts next to her while the strainer slipped back into the deep end.

Andy jumped up and raced to edge of the pool. "Spike's heading toward the drain!" he yelled. "We beat him!"

"You guys saved my life," Ellie said between coughs.

She closed her eyes thankfully and lay back in the grass. She'd never felt so exhausted in her life.

"He's totally gone," Andy reported from the pool.

Hans scrooched over to Ellie and put a hand on his sister's shoulder. "I'm glad you're okay, El."

She sat up and hugged Hans. "Me too, brat. Me too."

"Me three," Andy said. He walked over to Ellie and patted her awkwardly on the back.

"Thanks, Andy." Ellie felt suddenly shy. She'd never shared such a serious moment with her best friend, and the warm look in his eyes made her self-conscious.

"I thought you were a goner," Hans said.

"So did I," Ellie responded. She shuddered as she remembered Spike's cold grip. "I was about half a second away from drowning when you guys rescued me."

Andy flopped onto his back beside Ellie. "I can't believe we were so stupid."

"My thought exactly—as soon as I saw Spike next to me in the pool."

"Why were we stupid?" Hans asked.

"Because we didn't realize that a pool would be *just* the kind of place that Spike would love. He's most at home in the water, not to mention the huge drain," Andy explained.

"Jeez. I thought I'd be safe as long as I stayed out of the bathroom," Hans said.

"Nowhere's safe," Ellie said darkly.

"It might be time to tell your parents about Spike," Andy said. "We need help."

Ellie closed her eyes again. The late afternoon sun warmed her face, and she allowed the memory of Spike's red eyes to fade from her mind. "No way. You know how parents are."

"How are they?" Hans asked, sounding confused.

Ellie sighed. "There's no way they'll believe us. They'll end up thinking we're crazy, which will just make everything worse."

"If *that's* possible," Andy remarked dryly.

Before the sentence was even out of Andy's mouth, Ellie saw Spike's body beginning to slither out of the pool. He hadn't gone down the drain after all—he'd just been waiting for the right moment to attack again.

Ellie's exhaustion drained away as she jumped to her feet and grabbed the long silver pole of the pool strainer.

"I've had enough of this," Ellie shouted to Hans and Andy. "I'm getting him *now!*"

Before either boy could try to stop her, Ellie charged toward the side of the pool. Her fear had been replaced by deep, burning anger. She felt as strong as twelve Olympic athletes as she approached the monster and his beady red eyes.

When Ellie was just a foot away, the monster turned his head and flicked his tongue in the direction of Hans.

Putting every ounce of her weight behind the pole, Ellie stabbed Spike in the middle of his green, slime-covered body. The monster's head immediately rolled to one side, and a thick black ooze spurted from inside his stomach.

Ellie covered her mouth with one hand, resisting the urge to throw up. Slime continued to pour from the monster, who was now moaning and groaning with pain. Ellie watched, fascinated, as Spike sank to the bottom of the pool. A cloud of stench rose up around him, and Ellie gasped.

"Come look!" she called to Hans and Andy.

They ran to her side, eyes widening at the sight of the dying monster. All three stood silently as they watched Spike's motionless body float toward the drain of the pool. His thin body slowly disappeared down the pipes—forever.

"We're free!" Hans shouted, hugging Ellie tightly.

Ellie hugged her little brother back and gave Andy a high five.

"Well, I'll tell you both one thing," Ellie said, giggling with sheer relief.

"What?" Andy asked. He dropped onto the grass and propped himself up on his elbows.

"I'm not getting back into that pool for a long, long time."

From out of the corner of her eye Ellie thought she saw a sudden wave of purple bubbles shoot up from the drain at the bottom of the pool.

Get a grip, she told herself. *You're safe now.*

Chapter

17

"So, what did you two do this afternoon?" Mrs. Volkhausen asked as the family sat down to dinner.

"Watched TV," Ellie answered.

"Played soccer," Hans said at the same time.

Ellie kicked Hans under the table. "Ow!" he yelped.

"Hans and Andy played soccer. I watched TV." Ellie smiled innocently at her mother.

"I thought you were in hot pursuit of a new experiment," Mr. Volkhausen commented.

Ellie pictured Spike's long, slimy body and sharp teeth. She shook her head. "I'm, uh, kind of taking a break from chemistry right now," she stuttered. "Uh, can I have some more mashed potatoes, please?"

Mrs. Volkhausen passed the dish of potatoes. "You and Andy are sure spending a lot of time together."

Ellie rolled her eyes. "So?"

Out of the corner of her eye Ellie saw her mom wink at her dad. Nauseating! "Just a comment, sweetie," Mrs. Volkhausen said calmly.

"Ellie and Andy kissing in a tree," Hans sang. "K-I-S-S-I-N-G!"

Ellie kicked Hans again, harder this time. "Shut up, brat."

"Your brother's just teasing, honey," Mr. Volkhausen said.

"Can we please change the subject?" Ellie asked.

"Have you kids been in the pool?" Mr. Volkhausen asked, suddenly looking stern.

Be careful what you wish for, Ellie thought. The pool was the *last* subject she wanted to discuss. "No, Dad. Why?"

"The thing is filthy. There's some kind of scum all over the bottom of it."

Hans stared at his meat loaf while Ellie choked on her milk. She was almost tempted to tell her parents the absolute truth. *Mom and Dad, there was a murderous monster on the loose. He almost drowned me in the pool today.*

85

"Yeah, right," Ellie muttered to herself. There was no way in the world her parents would believe *that* story. They'd probably stick her in a mental institution, no questions asked.

"I asked if either of you knows what happened to the pool?" her father repeated, sounding suspicious.

Ellie sipped her milk, willing her heart to stop hammering. "Uh, no, Dad. I haven't been in the pool all week. Neither has Hans."

"Is that true?" Mr. Volkhausen asked Hans.

Ellie kicked her little brother, this time being careful not to make the impact so forceful that he cried out. "Yeah, Daddy. We haven't been in the pool for ages."

"I don't need to tell you two that you're not allowed in the pool without an adult present," Mrs. Volkhausen said firmly. "That goes for you too, Ellie. It's just not safe."

Ellie nodded, mentally groping for yet another topic of conversation. A topic that had less than nothing to do with Spike. Unfortunately she blurted out the first thing that came to mind.

"So, uh, Mom, I decided to take that dancing class you were talking about the other day," Ellie stuttered.

Mrs. Volkhausen's face lit up, and she beamed

at her daughter. "Ellie, this is wonderful. You're going to be such a darling dancer. I remember when I was your age . . . "

Ellie tuned out as her mother droned on and on about the glory days of junior high. Why had she offered to take that dumb class?

Ellie drowned her mashed potatoes in fresh gravy and stared gloomily at her plate. She had a sudden vision of herself trapped under a giant mound of potatoes, gravy dripping down to fill her nose and lungs. A frightened gasp escaped her mouth.

Calm down, she ordered herself. *He's dead. The monster can't ever hurt you again.* Still, the memory of Spike's death grip made her palms sweat and her heart race.

"Ellie, what's wrong, hon?" Mr. Volkhausen asked quickly.

Ellie managed a grim smile. "I was just picturing myself doing the foxtrot and the cha-cha-cha," she joked.

And dying, she added silently. *Dying a long and painful death.*

Chapter

By Friday afternoon Ellie felt totally drained of energy. She'd woken up at four in the morning after another nightmare about turning into a fish.

Then she'd stared at her ceiling until dawn, telling herself over and over that the danger was past. Spike was dead—the nightmare had been just an ugly reminder of their terrifying experience.

Now, as they headed toward home, Ellie felt awash with relief. As tired as she was, she couldn't wait to get home. The knowledge that Spike was gone made the Volkhausens' house seem like paradise.

"TGIF," Ellie said to Hans. "I thought Friday would never get here."

When Hans didn't respond, Ellie turned to look at her brother. They were a few blocks away from Grover Elementary, where Ellie picked up Hans every day. Usually she couldn't get him to shut up during their walk home. But today Hans was oddly silent.

"What's up, brat? Someone use your tongue in an art project at school?"

He shook his head. When he turned to look at her, Ellie saw fear in her brother's eyes. "I'm scared to go home," he said in a small voice.

Ellie sighed. "Everything will be fine, Hans. Spike has said his last good-bye."

"Why can't we go to Andy's?" Hans asked. "Just until Mom and Dad get home."

"He has to go to the orthodontist," Ellie answered. "His braces need to get tightened."

Hans wrinkled his nose. "Doesn't that hurt?"

Not as much as being strangled by a cold-blooded monster, she answered silently. Then she forced the thought from her mind. "It's not so bad, I guess. He says he's used to it."

Hans nodded as if he were extremely interested in Andy's braces. But Ellie could tell that he was just trying to be brave. His eyes were brimming with unshed tears, and his lower lip was trembling.

Ellie slung her arm around her brother's

shoulders, feeling a familiar surge of protectiveness. "We're one hundred percent monster-free now. Remember?"

Hans glanced at her hopefully. "Yeah, we are . . . "

"So forget the whole thing and go back to being a normal, pesky seven-year-old." Ellie gave Hans a soft punch on the arm.

"But how do you know he *really* died?" Hans asked. "Maybe he was faking."

"I just know," Ellie answered. "Once you're twelve, you know that kind of stuff."

Hans frowned slightly. "I guess everything'll be okay, then."

They rounded the corner, and the Volkhausens' house came into view. From half a block away the home seemed picture perfect. Ellie had to admit that it was hard to believe a monster had ever lurked inside.

"We'll do the laundry for Mom and make spaghetti for dinner," Ellie said, as if she were talking about a regular afternoon. "If you don't *completely* annoy me, I'll help you build a pillow fort in the den."

Hans smiled for the first time since leaving Grover Elementary. "Really?"

"If, and only if, you help me with the laundry," Ellie answered.

"All right!"

By the time they reached their front walk, Ellie had almost convinced herself that the last few days had been part of a long-ago nightmare.

Still, it couldn't hurt to let Hans feel they were being cautious. Just for today. If he felt they were being careful, he wouldn't be jumping at every little creak and groan of the house.

"Two rules when we get inside," Ellie said.

Hans's face fell. "What are they?"

"Number one, don't go near the pool. Number two, pee out in the backyard. Let's not go into the bathrooms until Mom or Dad gets home."

Hans grinned. "Cool! It'll be just like camping."

"Sure," Ellie whispered. "Just like camping on Halloween night with an escaped serial killer in the area."

But Hans didn't hear her. He'd already run ahead, his earlier fears apparently forgotten. *The monster is dead,* Ellie repeated to herself. *He can never hurt us again.*

But as she reached for her key, Ellie wished she *felt* as sure about that fact as she sounded.

Chapter

19

"**G**et the light," Ellie told Hans.

Her arms were aching under the weight of twenty pounds of dirty laundry, and the moss green plastic laundry basket was digging painfully into the side of her left hip.

"I hate the basement," Hans said, hesitating outside the door.

Ellie shifted the basket. "Please, Hans. My arms are about to fall off."

He opened the basement door and flipped the light switch on the wall. Then he moved back into the kitchen. "You go first."

Ellie made her way carefully down the stairs. She couldn't see over the huge mound of laundry, and with every step she imagined herself tumbling headfirst down the steep flight of stairs. At last she reached the bottom.

"You can come down now," she called to Hans, who was still standing in the doorway. "Everything's fine down here."

With a relieved sigh, Ellie plunked down the laundry next to the washing machine. After rubbing her sore biceps for a few moments Ellie dumped out the dirty clothes and began separating the whites from the colors.

"You're sure Spike isn't down here?" Hans asked, appearing at her side.

Ellie took another glance around the room. There were piles of cardboard boxes, old furniture, and toys scattered around the floor. In the corner was the furnace, as well as her dad's seldom used tool bench. Everything was exactly as she'd last seen it.

"Look for yourself," she said. "The most dangerous thing down here is the overpowering smell of mildew."

Hans took a few steps away from her. His gaze traveled across all four corners of the basement. Finally he turned to Ellie and grinned. "Just a boring basement, with boring laundry."

Ellie knelt next to the big pile of laundry. "Yep. Now give me a hand with the boring shirts and pants."

For the next few minutes Ellie and Hans separated the laundry in comfortable silence. After several days of Spike's reign of terror, performing such a routine chore was almost fun.

"Let's put the colors in first," Ellie said.

She turned the washing machine on COLD, the way her mom had taught her, and let the water begin to fill the deep cavity of the machine.

"Should I put the clothes in?" Hans asked.

"In a minute." Ellie reached for a box of powdered detergent that Mrs. Volkhausen had left on a table next to the dryer. She looked into the box. "Shoot. There's not even enough in here for one load. I'll have to get a fresh box from the pantry."

"Do I have to do anything?" Hans asked, eyeing the pile of brightly colored clothes.

"When the machine gets close to half full, put in the clothes. I'll be right back."

In the kitchen pantry Ellie grabbed a new box of detergent and then reached for a box of fabric softener. As she stood upright, her hands full, Ellie heard a muffled wail from the direction of the basement.

She froze, and the detergent and fabric softener slipped from her fingers. She knew instantly why Hans was screaming. As impossible as it seemed, Spike had lived through her violent attack.

Now Hans was in trouble—again. And Ellie didn't even have Andy to help her protect Hans. She was on her own.

Her heart pounded as she came to her senses and sprang into action. Ellie grabbed a broom from the corner of the pantry to use as a weapon and raced to the door of the basement.

She leapt down the steps two at a time, not even caring if she ended up falling. She had to get to the bottom—fast.

Ellie saw the monster before she saw her brother. Most of Spike's long, puke-green body was wound around the washing machine. Slime oozed from the gash that remained on his body from Ellie's stab.

His huge jaw was wide open, revealing his sharp teeth. Ellie trembled as she remembered how close those same fangs had been to her face just yesterday.

Ellie stepped into the shadows near the stairs. She figured that the only advantage she *might* get over Spike was the element of surprise. Once he caught sight of her, she'd be an easy target.

Trying to steady her breathing, Ellie's eyes sought out Hans. For several seconds she couldn't see him. *Maybe he's hiding,* she told herself. She couldn't allow herself to imagine the other possibility—that Spike had already killed and maybe eaten her little brother.

Then she saw him. Hans was *inside* the washing machine. He was almost totally hidden by the monster's waving tentacles, but Ellie finally saw a patch of her brother's long-sleeved yellow T-shirt.

"Help me!" Hans screamed.

The sudden noise seemed to surprise Spike. The creature slithered to the concrete floor, whipping his long tail back and forth. He raised most of his body in the air, balancing on his wide, slimy fins.

"Ellie, help me," Hans wailed again. His voice was shrill and desperate.

Finally Ellie had a full view of her brother. His legs and part of his upper body were in the washing machine, which was spilling over with water. His hair was dripping wet, and Ellie was sure that tears were mingled with the water on his bright red cheeks.

One of the monster's tentacles was wrapped around Hans's neck. Another tentacle rested on top of the washing machine lid. Ellie knew that Spike could literally squeeze the life out of Hans within a matter of seconds. Water poured from the washing machine, spilling onto the floor.

Ellie longed to call out to Hans and let him know she was nearby but stopped herself. She had to approach the situation with science and reason. If she panicked, both she and her brother were doomed.

"Stay cool, Hans," she whispered. "I've got a plan." *Not a good plan,* she added silently. *But it's better than nothing.*

The monster began to thrash Hans from side to side. Water continued to gush over the sides of the washing machine. By now Ellie was standing in a pool of water. Almost the entire floor of the basement was covered. Strangled gasps escaped from Hans.

Ellie took a deep breath, then lifted the handle of the broom high above her head.

One, two, three . . .

Chapter

Ellie sprinted out of the shadows, screaming like a madwoman and waving the broom. As she'd hoped, the movement startled the creature.

Spike turned his head away from Hans's frightened face. For what seemed like the millionth time Ellie found herself staring into the monster's blazing red eyes. *Stay calm,* Ellie ordered herself.

"Ellie!" Hans croaked tearfully.

Spike came toward her on his finlike feet. As the monster moved away from the washing machine his tentacle unwound from around Hans's neck.

From the corner of her eye Ellie saw Hans slump farther into the machine, gasping for breath. For now, at least, he was alive.

"Hans, get out of there!" she screamed.

Then, using every ounce of her strength, Ellie swung the broom handle at Spike's head. But in the tenth of a second before the wood struck, Ellie realized that she'd made a mistake.

The monster could move lightning quick when he wanted to. He moved his head a fraction of an inch as the handle came close. His jaw closed around the wood, snapping the broom in two.

Ellie looked down at her hand. Her weapon was now no more than a pile of straw and a short, splintered end of a broom handle. Her gaze moved from the useless broom to Spike's hideous face.

Ellie was sure she saw a sneer form on his face. The monster advanced lazily, forcing Ellie to creep backward.

When her back hit the cold basement wall, she froze. She was trapped, just as Hans had been. Mocking her with his glowing red eyes, the monster reached out and flicked Ellie's face with a slimy green tentacle.

Ellie's cheek stung sharply where he'd struck her. She put a shaking hand to her face, feeling her heart pounding painfully in her chest. She knew she should try to run, but her muscles felt frozen.

Spike's body stiffened suddenly, and his thin, blood-red tongue shot out of his mouth. With a loud hiss he lunged at Ellie.

"Duck!" Hans shouted from across the room.

Ellie flung herself to the floor, adrenaline pumping through her veins. The monster groaned angrily as his head missed Ellie's and slammed against the hard wall.

Ellie sprang into action. She crawled away from the wall on her hands and knees, moving faster than she'd ever thought possible.

"Over here!" Hans called. He was standing in the one dry corner of the basement, behind a cluttered table. In one hand he held their father's ball peen hammer.

Ellie scrambled to her feet. She darted toward the table, the monster at her heels. One of Spike's fins bumped against the back of her knees.

She heard the monster's delighted hiss as she fell. Ellie's stomach banged against the metal table. Objects on the table flew in every direction. A huge old fan fell on Hans's toe and he shouted out with pain.

Ellie tried to regain her balance but failed. Her head smacked against the concrete floor. Before she knew what happened, she was sprawled on her back, looking up at Spike's looming head.

Her ears rang from the throbbing in her head. From what seemed like a million miles away, Ellie heard a gentle whirring. She closed her eyes, fighting back waves of pain.

She finally opened her eyes again, dreading what she knew she'd see—Spike's elastic jaw, ready to clamp down on her arms, legs, or head.

But the monster wasn't even looking at her. His beady eyes were turned in the direction of the corner. Ellie lifted her aching neck and followed Spike's gaze.

She saw immediately what had the monster so entranced. Hans. Her little brother still held the hammer in one hand. With the other he was holding the huge fan like a shield in front of him. He looked fierce and dangerous—totally unlike the scrawny seven-year-old she was used to.

"Get back here now!" Hans yelled. Ellie could tell from the strain in his voice that he was having a tough time holding up the heavy fan. She was surprised that the thing had stayed plugged in through its fall. Now the loud noise of the whirring blades broke the tense silence in the basement.

She rolled under the table and came out on the other side. When she stood, the monster was still staring at Hans, his eyes wide and his pupils dilated. Spike's mouth hung open and drool dripped from between his fleshy lips. Ellie grabbed the fan from Hans and held it with both hands.

"Get behind me," she ordered.

Spike moved a few feet backward, where the floor was still covered with water from the washing machine. All of a sudden Ellie realized why the monster hadn't yet attacked.

The air from the fan was drying out his scales, weakening his awesome strength. Ellie watched as the monster slithered to the wet floor. He stretched out his body so that it was pencil thin, obviously trying to cover himself in water.

"Let's run, *now*," Ellie whispered to Hans.

Hans didn't need to be told twice. He bolted across the basement floor. Ellie yanked the fan's plug from the wall socket and followed Hans, gasping for breath.

They were halfway up the basement stairs before the monster noticed. He reared up, letting out a groan that made Ellie's blood run cold. "Keep going," she said, giving Hans a quick nudge.

Hans flung open the basement door and tumbled into the kitchen. The hammer skidded across the kitchen linoleum, then clanged against the leg of a chair. Hans started to go after it.

"Forget that!" Ellie shouted. "We've got to get this fan plugged in."

Hans grabbed the cord and pushed the plug into a socket next to the basement door. Ellie switched the fan on HIGH and then stood in the doorway of the basement.

Spike was several feet below her on the stairs. When the cool air started blowing onto him full force, he bared his fangs and flicked his tongue.

Ellie was terrified, but she held her ground. She had no choice. After several seconds Spike's head lolled back and forth and his red eyes became dull.

Finally the monster slid slowly down the stairs. Ellie climbed down as far as the cord would reach and held her breath.

As she'd hoped, Spike made his way to the washing machine. Stretching himself thin one more time, he disappeared down a rubber tube that hung from one side of the machine.

Ellie went back up the stairs and slammed the basement door. Exhausted, she sank to the floor. Hans stood next to her, the hammer in his hand once again.

Ellie stared up at her brother's scared face. "I know how we're going to kill the monster," she said in a grim voice. "But I'll need your help."

Chapter

21

Saturday morning Ellie heaved a sigh of relief as she shut and locked the front door behind her parents. They were going to a conference in another town and wouldn't be back until evening. Plenty of time to put her plan into action and kill Spike. Or get killed, depending on whether or not the plan worked.

"Remember, tomorrow is family day," her mother had said just before walking out the door. *Sure,* Ellie had thought. *If the family is still alive tomorrow.*

Ellie turned to Andy, who'd arrived a few minutes before her parents had left. "Ready for show time?" she asked.

He raised his eyebrows skeptically. "You still

haven't explained exactly how we're going to work this thing," he said.

"Come up to my room and I'll show you." Ellie took the stairs two at a time, anxious to show off the invention she'd worked on late into the night.

Hans was waiting in Ellie's room, a worried frown on his face. "I'm the bait," he said to Andy.

"Bait? Are we going fishing?" Andy asked.

Ellie laughed dryly. "That's one way of putting it."

She led Andy to the card table she'd set up in the middle of her room. On its surface were three hair dryers. Three very *unusual* hair dryers. Ellie picked one up, holding it proudly.

"Voilà! I present the Instamatic, battery-operated, monster-destroying hair dryer." She waved the dryer in front of her like a sword.

She'd refashioned the everyday hair dryers so that each was battery powered, with extra voltage. Without the need for a wall socket they could take the dryers anywhere in the house.

"Cool!" Hans exclaimed, reaching for another.

Andy made a small bow. "As usual, you're a genius. But what's the point?"

Ellie wiggled her eyebrows. "Hans and I realized yesterday that our only real defense against Spike is good old air."

"Air?" Andy asked, sounding surprised.

"Yep. The one thing a fish, a *monster* fish, cannot live without for more than a few minutes is water."

"So?" Andy picked up the third hair dryer as if it were a lethal weapon.

"So we're going to dry him to death. Simple. I can't believe I didn't think of it before."

Hans squinted at Ellie. "But won't Spike get himself wet, the way he did yesterday? Then slither back down the pipes?"

Ellie opened her mouth to answer, but her words were cut off by the doorbell. "Aha! There's Larry Lobo."

"That buffoon?" Andy yelled. "How's he going to help?"

"He's got the solution to Hans's question," Ellie shouted over her shoulder. She was already out the door of her room and heading down the stairs.

Larry, wearing a bright pink jumpsuit with a cursive *L* stitched over his heart, entered the foyer. Andy and Hans quickly followed Ellie through the hallway.

"Hi, y'all," Larry said cheerfully. "Sorry our little mission didn't turn out better the other day."

"Don't worry about it," Ellie said. "That's all in the past. I just need you to do me one more favor." She paused. "Well, two favors."

"Be glad to, little lady. Are you wanting to go down in the sewer again?"

Ellie shook her head. "Not exactly." She turned to Andy and Hans, a gleam in her eye. "Larry is going to shut off our main water valve. We'll have no water. Period. If you get my drift."

"Ellie, you're truly brilliant," Andy said, grinning.

Ellie looked Andy in the eye. "Let's just hope you think so two hours from now. When Larry comes over to turn the water valve back on."

Let's just hope we're still here—and breathing—when he comes back, she added silently.

Chapter

Twenty minutes later Larry Lobo had completed his task. He left with a promise to return in exactly two hours.

Andy sat at the kitchen table, an unopened bag of potato chips in front of him. "I'm glad you didn't ask Looney Larry to stick around. He would have botched our plan for sure."

Ellie had been pacing back and forth, going over the details of the next hour in her mind. She stopped mid-stride to agree with her friend. "You read my mind, Andy. This is something we've got to do on our own."

Hans slouched in his seat. "I'm the bait," he repeated for the hundredth time in the last half an hour.

Ellie ruffled her brother's blond curls. "Andy and I will be there the whole time. We'll protect you."

"Yeah, bud, you've got the fun part," Andy said.

Ellie appreciated the confidence in his voice, although she was sure it was for Hans's benefit. She was certain that under his calm exterior Andy was as petrified as she was.

"Okay, then. Let's do it," Ellie said.

They gathered in the upstairs bathroom, where Spike had made his first appearance as a monster.

Hans climbed into the carefully dried-out bathtub, wearing only his swim trunks and an old set of scuba gear. He'd insisted on the face mask and breathing tube just in case something went wrong. At his side was one of the portable hair dryers.

"I'm ready," Hans called from the tub.

"Great. Andy and I will be just outside the door," Ellie said.

There was a rumbling from deep in the pipes. Ellie knew from her plumbing research that the pipes were still filled with leftover water. Spike would have no trouble getting into the house.

"I hope you really know what you're doing," Andy whispered as they crouched behind the closed bathroom door.

"I don't," Ellie whispered back. "But this is the only chance we've got."

"Ssh. I hear something," Andy said.

They pressed their ears to the door. Ellie's heart was beating a thousand beats a second in her chest, and she felt as if she might throw up at any second. But she pushed her fear aside, knowing that her actions would have to safeguard Hans's life.

On the other side of the door she heard a loud hiss. She heard the distinct sound of a large jaw being snapped open and shut. Ellie felt time stop. "Now, Hans!" she shouted.

Inside the bathroom the loud motor of the blow dryer started up. "Get in position," she whispered to Andy.

Ellie counted slowly to five, then flung open the bathroom door. The monster was staring her right in the eyes.

"Ready, aim, fire!" she screamed at Andy.

They switched on their hair dryers, sending hot streams of air directly into Spike's face. The monster groaned loudly, whipping his body from side to side. Behind him Hans was standing upright in the bathtub, clutching his hair dryer with both hands.

"Now turn it off," she whispered loudly to Andy. This was the stage of her plan that had worried her most. They had to lure the monster out of the bathroom so that Hans could get out safely.

Andy and Ellie turned off their dryers and began backing down the hallway. Hans kept his on, carefully aiming the nozzle at the back of Spike's head. His body blocked the toilet and sink, making it impossible for the creature to escape.

The monster slid out of the bathroom, seeming desperate to get away from Hans's weapon. Ellie and Andy continued down the hallway.

Ellie kept her eyes on Spike, knowing that he could strike with one of his tentacles at any moment. "Hans, now!" she shouted.

Her brother flew out of the bathroom. Spike turned and reached for him, but he was a second too late. Hans raced away from Ellie and Andy, heading for the back stairs as they'd planned. So far, so good.

Ellie was so intent on the monster's writhing body that she'd forgotten Andy was supposed to be beside her. She remembered him a moment later when she heard a loud thump followed by a pained cry.

Ellie turned her head quickly. Andy had backed up so far down the hall that he'd reached the front stairs. Then he had taken one step too many and tumbled down the stairs.

"It's just you and me," Ellie said to the monster.

She could see that he was losing strength. His body was moving slowly, and his eyes had glazed over to a dull red. She allowed him to get closer to her.

"Three, two, one," Ellie said aloud. She held the dryer in front of her and switched the ON button.

But nothing happened. Ellie flipped the switch again. The appliance was dead in her hands. Completely and totally useless.

One of Spike's tentacles shot out and wrapped around her arm. The hair dryer dropped to the ground as Ellie struggled against the monster's pull.

But Ellie was powerless. Even in his weakened state Spike was ten times stronger than she was.

Ellie almost fainted when she felt the cold hardness of the monster's teeth. She screamed. . .

Chapter

Spike's jaw clamped shut, and Ellie waited for the waves of pain. But when she looked down at her arm, she saw that his teeth had closed around the loose material of the sleeve of her flannel shirt. She yanked away her arm, hearing the sound of ripping material as she freed herself.

"Hold on, Ellie, I'm coming," Hans yelled from down the hall.

Ellie fought Spike, bracing her feet against his body. Again his jaw was just millimeters away. This time he'd be sure to get his mouth firmly around her skin.

But the sound of Hans's hair dryer came closer, and Spike dropped Ellie from his hold. The monster turned around and began to slither down the hallway.

Ellie jumped up. "He's trying to get away!"

"But he can't go down the pipes," Hans shouted.

Ellie grabbed her brother's hair dryer and followed Spike. The monster's long, snot-green body left a trail of slime as he made his way down the hallway.

"Larry told me it takes at least half an hour for the pipes to drain," she yelled. "He can still escape!"

Spike was just a couple of feet from the bathroom door now. He stretched his body so that his head reached almost to the ceiling of the hallway. High above their heads Spike's jaw opened and closed quickly. His pointed tongue flicked back and forth as quick as lightning, reminding Ellie of how he'd stung her cheek in the laundry room.

Scared as she was, Ellie pushed herself to go forward. In just a few seconds Spike could be into the bathroom and down the pipes. Ellie ran faster, holding the dryer out as far as she could.

When Spike was just a foot from the door, Andy materialized from the back stairs, holding a dryer in one hand. He leapt toward the door, reaching for the knob with his free hand.

Ellie shouted triumphantly as Andy's hand closed around the doorknob. He pulled the door shut with a bang that echoed through the house. "Yes!" Ellie cried, sprinting forward.

The monster heaved his body toward the door, then sagged to the floor. Andy turned on his dryer and took a few steps back.

Ellie neared him, her dryer going full blast. They were just beyond the monster's reach, blasting him with air. Ellie felt Hans come up behind her. She put her free arm around his shoulders, hugging him close to her side. "It's almost over," she whispered weakly.

The monster's movements became more and more jerky. Finally he stopped moving altogether. He lay in a scaly, hideous heap, his eyes closed.

Still, they kept the air currents aimed at his body. Ellie didn't want to take any chances. She smiled as Spike's body began to shrivel up, getting smaller and smaller.

His scales peeled from his body and fell in flakes to the carpet. The slime green of his fins turned to an ashy gray, and his tongue hung limply from his jaw.

After several minutes the monster was nothing more than a pile of dead skin and sharp teeth. "He's dead!" Andy yelled.

Ellie turned off her hair dryer and let it hang at her side. At last the nightmare was over. A deep sense of relief swept through her as she realized that they were all truly safe now.

"What are we going to do with him?" Hans asked, studying the remains of the monster's body.

Ellie laughed. "I'll tell you what we're *not* going to do."

"What's that?" Andy asked.

"Flush him down the toilet," Ellie responded, grinning.

Hans picked up one of the creature's fangs. "Can we bury him in the backyard, the way I wanted to all along?" he asked.

"Great idea," Andy said, giving Hans a high five.

Ellie hugged her little brother. "You know, for a seven-year-old you're not so dumb."

She scooped up the flaky ashes, which were all that remained of Spike, then started toward the back stairs. "When we're done, I'll make a round of my special banana and grilled cheese sandwiches," she said.

"Yeah!" Hans yelled.

Ellie turned around and smiled at her brother, then her best friend. "You guys deserve something special today," she said quietly. "We all do."

Chapter

24

When Hans and Ellie got home from school on Monday afternoon, Ellie was surprised to find her mother already there.

"Why aren't you at work?" Ellie asked, throwing her backpack on the kitchen table.

"The boss gave us all the afternoon off," she replied, pulling a tray of her special caramel brownies out of the oven.

"That's great, Mom," Ellie said as Hans ran over and hugged his mother around the waist. "I hope you've been relaxing."

Mrs. Volkhausen nodded. "Mostly. Although I did have to do a little cleaning. There was the most horrendous smell coming from your room, Ellie."

Ellie gulped. She'd left an experiment out overnight, hoping for an interesting reaction. "Oops."

"Yes, oops. I know you're determined to win the Nobel Prize, but this particular experiment got flushed down the toilet."

"Sorry, Mom," Ellie said.

Hans squeezed past Mrs. Volkhausen to get to the brownies. "Just one," she said.

Then Mrs. Volkhausen crossed the kitchen and tugged gently on Ellie's arm. Ellie followed her mother into the hall, wondering if she was going to get a harsher lecture about having left the chemicals out all night and day.

"I really am sorry, Mom—" Ellie started.

Mrs. Volkhausen smiled. "This isn't about the stink in your room, honey. Although it was pretty horrendous."

"What is it, then?" Ellie asked. Had her mother somehow found out about the fish monster? Had Hans spilled the beans when she wasn't around?

"It's Hans's fish," Mrs. Volkhausen said.

Ellie gulped. "Uh, what about him?" she asked, her voice little more than a squeak.

"Well, when I came home this afternoon, Spike II was dead. I found him floating at the top of his fishbowl."

Ellie nodded, waiting for her mother to continue.

"Anyway, I went to the pet store and got a replacement. So don't let on if you notice a difference in the fishes."

Ellie felt a slow sinking sensation in her chest. "Uh, what did you do with Spike II?" she asked.

"I flushed him," Mrs. Volkhausen answered. Then she patted Ellie on the head and stepped back into the kitchen.

Ellie stood staring at the wall, feeling almost dizzy. Her mother had flushed both Spike II *and* the chemicals down the toilet.

But what were the chances of the same reaction happening again? Anyway, the chemicals were different. Totally different.

Ellie nodded to herself. There was nothing to worry about. Absolutely nothing at all. *So why do I feel like throwing up?* she wondered miserably.

Chapter

25

Tuesday evening Ellie and Andy arrived at the Volkhausens' front door. They'd just completed their first dancing lesson. The sun was sinking slowly in the sky, and from inside Ellie could smell the delicious aroma of her mother's fried chicken.

At last life was back to normal. There had been no strange rumbling in the pipes since the death of Spike II, and Ellie was convinced that the danger was over.

"Well, uh, thanks for walking me home," Ellie said.

"No prob. I mean, you're welcome," Andy responded.

"You really didn't need to do it," she said.

Andy stared at the ground and scuffed one of his brand-new penny loafers against the brick of the Volkhausens' walkway. Finally he glanced up and shrugged. "I guess it's a Miss Manners thing. You know, walking a girl home after a dance and all that."

"Who cares about Miss Manners? Personally I'd rather spend the evening doing chemistry experiments," Ellie said.

Andy laughed. "Come on, the foxtrot was kind of cool." He moved his feet in a little box step. "You think I have the makings of the next Fred Astaire? Or Michael Jackson?"

Ellie giggled. "Hardly."

"Maybe I should take up kick boxing instead," Andy said, punching the air with closed fists.

Ellie kicked her left leg high, giggling again. "Sounds good to me. Let's try to convince our moms."

Ellie did another kick, then turned to look at Andy. He hadn't responded to her last comment.

"What's wrong?" she asked.

"Look over there," Andy said, sounding as if he'd just seen a ghost.

"What?" Ellie glanced in the direction that Andy was pointing.

Her mouth dropped open, and she froze.

Halfway down the block a big, brightly painted van was parked in front of her neighbors, the Alsups', house. LARRY LOBO'S UNUSUAL PLUMBING SERVICES was painted in neon green across one side.

"This can't be happening," Andy said, his voice barely above a whisper.

Ellie swallowed hard. "It *is* happening," she said. "Spike II is back."

BONE CHILLERS

This collection of spine-tingling horrors will scare you silly!
Be sure not to miss any of these eerie tales.

#1: BEWARE THE SHOPPING MALL
#2: LITTLE PET SHOP OF HORRORS
#3: BACK TO SCHOOL
#4: FRANKENTURKEY
#5: STRANGE BREW
#6: TEACHER CREATURE
#7: FRANKENTURKEY II
#8: WELCOME TO ALIEN INN
#9 ATTACK OF THE KILLER ANTS
#10 SLIME TIME
#11 TOILET TERROR*
#12 NIGHT OF THE LIVING CLAY*

* coming soon

TUNE IN YOUR TV TO ABC THIS FALL AND WATCH

BONE CHILLERS

ON SATURDAY MORNINGS

HarperPaperbacks

Look for

BONE CHILLERS

the new TV series on ABC this fall, Saturdays at 10:30 A.M., Eastern time. Check your local listings . . .

and prepare to be
SCARED!